ABOUT

MW00638544

Bronwyn Donaghy is a journalist who has been a specialist writer on family and children's issues for the past eighteen years. Her articles and columns appear regularly in *The Sydney Morning Herald*, *Parents Magazine*, *New Woman*, *Family Circle*, *Sydney's Child* and many other publications. She published a novel for children in 1994. *Anna's Story* is her first adult book. Bronwyn has been married for twenty-two years and has three teenage children.

By the same author

Keeping Mum
Leaving Early
Unzipped

ANNA'S STORY

BRONWYN DONAGHY

Angus&Robertson
An imprint of HarperCollins*Publishers*

Angus&Robertson
An imprint of HarperCollins*Publishers*, Australia

First published in Australia in 1996
Reprinted in 1996 (twice), 1997 (twice), 1998, 1999 (twice),
2000 (three times), 2001 (twice)
by HarperCollins*Publishers* Pty Limited
ABN 36 009 913 517
A member of the HarperCollins*Publishers* (Australia) Pty Limited Group
www.harpercollins.com.au

HarperCollins*Publishers*
25 Ryde Road, Pymble, Sydney NSW 2073, Australia
31 View Road, Glenfield, Auckland 10, New Zealand
77–85 Fulham Palace Road, London W6 8JB, United Kingdom
Hazelton Lanes, 55 Avenue Road, Suite 2900, Toronto, Ontario M5R 3L2
and 1995 Markham Road, Scarborough, Ontario M1B 5M8, Canada
10 East 53rd Street, New York NY 10022, USA

National Library of Australia Cataloguing-in-Publication data:

Donaghy, Bronwyn, 1948– .
Anna's story.
ISBN 0 207 19184 0.
1. Wood, Anna – Death and burial. 2. Drug abuse – Australia – Biography.
3. Youth – Drug abuse – Australia – Prevention.
4. Drug abuse – Study and teaching – Australia. I. Title.
362.29170994

Cover design by Darian Causby, HarperCollins Design Studio
Printed and bound in Australia by Griffin Press on 80gsm Econoprint

16 15 14 13   01 02 03 04

This book is dedicated
to the memory of Anna Victoria Wood 1980 – 1995

And to my family, with love

CONTENTS

FOREWORD

I had misgivings about this book when I heard that it was being written so soon after Anna's death. About the rekindling of grief it would bring for her bereaved family. About the media hype it would again provoke about one young drug-related death among so many. But now, I am so glad that Bronwyn Donaghy has brought us this moving tribute to Anna's short life and to her family's courage in sharing her story. *Anna's Story* is current, thought-provoking, relevant, inspiring and very very sad.

Anna's Story is about a marvellous young person, cruelly snatched from life in her nubile prime. It is a story of our time, told simply and powerfully by people who knew Anna well. And by Anna herself through her poems and letters. Surprisingly perhaps, there are no harsh judgements here. But anguish, heartache, pain, wry humour — yes. *Anna's Story* is about a beautiful young woman who should not have died. Not like this. Not from a single, whole ecstasy tablet.

My wife, Anne, and I have four children. Lisa, Adam and Sari have made it to their twenties and are reaching out to maturity, each in their own special way. But our youngest is sixteen years old, an age mate of the late Anna Wood. Nathan sounds a bit like her, actually — outgoing, exuberant, fun-loving and popular. He tells me things about the kids of today. For example (speaking of others, I dearly hope): "It's normal for kids of my age to experiment a bit with drugs." Followed by: "Anyway, you're the expert, Dad. You're supposed to know these things." My older kids tell me that we would be horrified by some of the things that they got up to at Nathan's age. No doubt we would.

Adolescent risk-taking, in particular drug use and abuse, has become very topical for parents of the 1990s. In discussions that

I have from time to time with groups of parents, this subject always comes up, together with rising teenage suicide rates. As a source of major concern to parents, it overshadows even adolescent sexuality, probably because (as Bronwyn Donaghy explains), we are dealing with a new phenomenon. The prospect of modern, adolescent drug-taking is terrifying to us because we have so little understanding of it. But we do know that it's extremely dangerous — Anna's untimely death has been like a punch to the communal gut in that regard.

The unedited draft of *Anna's Story* arrived in a big envelope one weekday in mid-March. The following weekend, I couldn't put it down. Lying in bed, I was too moved to read it out loud. *Anna's Story* is, after all, real life. Angela, Tony and Alice Wood are people we have come to know. We wonder, along with them, what they might have done differently. Why did this tragedy happen to them? Why couldn't it happen to us?

For me, the most important message that comes through in this poignant book is that we, as parents, urgently need to become empowered as advocates for our children's safe behaviour. More effective than any academic report, *Anna's Story* lifts the lid off teenage drug-taking and drug-peddling. It strips away the transparent glamour from rave/ecstasy parties and about even "staying overnight at a friend's place". It highlights the vexed issue of "parental trust versus teenage freedom". These days, we do need to check things out. We need to ask questions and to clearly establish accountability, as best we can, in relation to our children's actions and whereabouts.

But of course, even this does not provide a failsafe antidote to dangerous adolescent risk-taking. In any given situation, the decision-maker is the young person alone. For that reason, *Anna's Story* is also for teenagers. Bronwyn Donaghy, herself a concerned parent, talks to kids directly in a chapter entitled "Just for Kids". It's about *poison*! It asks provocative questions. It makes you think.

In a report on the Youth Forum, chaired by Alice Wood, kids speak out themselves on the issue of drug education. They ask to be heard and they want to take action. They ask for our support and they throw the challenge at our feet. As a professional devoted to the health and medical care of young people, I am immensely pleased that the Australian Medical Associaton has mounted the Anna Wood Drug and Alcohol Education Project. This is an important, timely and (with adequate public support) ongoing initiative.

Finally, you should be aware that *Anna's Story* is not a light read. It is intensely, often discomfortingly personal, as it needs to be. I warmly recommend this book to Australian parents and their teenage children. It could save the life of someone you love.

David Bennett AO MBBS FRACP
Head, Department of Adolescent Medicine
The New Children's Hospital, Westmead, NSW

Member of Expert Committee
Anna Wood Drug and Alcohol Education Project

A MESSAGE FROM KATE CEBERANO

When I first heard about Anna Wood my blood went cold and I had an overwhelming feeling that I had somehow been responsible for this tragedy. I have known for a long time, it seems, what other children have not had the good fortune to know. That drugs, one way or another, kill! By kill I don't exactly just mean one's mortality. I mean one's initiative, one's ambitions and dreams, and most importantly, one's mind.

I was brought up believing my mind was my only weapon against mediocrity (a state or level of life abhorrent to me). With all faculties intact I could reach into my imagination and draw inspiration for life. You need to be inspired to live because life is hard! Drugs do not make it easier. For every synthetic glimpse of nirvana you have, you lose from your natural resources.

My confession is that, at times, whilst knowing what I know, I have remained somewhat mute, not wishing to offend or seem like some nerdy wowser. But now I have to speak out for Anna and for my friends who are daily struggling with paranoia, fear and addiction, and who may be dancing dangerously in some carefully contrived illusion that it's okay to experiment, it's only normal, it can't hurt you.

I don't believe that propagating safe usage of drugs is the solution. Apart from this being naive, it's promoting the idea that one can use drugs sensibly. Excuse me, but drugs are *insensible*. Their main purpose is to alter and disturb the natural perception of the mind.

A new strategy for governments to handle this would be to create community projects that restore family support and get younger people employed, stimulated and busy.

I think people in this country generally are quite shy. I have observed that drugs are often used as a method of covering up social or personal inadequacies. The true value of a person is based on the accuracy with which *they* can communicate what *they* feel and think!

Drugs can occlude this ability, sometimes temporarily, sometimes permanently. I find this very sad and very frustrating.

I would like to personally organise seminars on the subject of communication and encourage understanding of where this problem really begins.

One does have a choice, and the way we make choices that mean survival is by being totally informed. That can mean the difference between being totally duped and dead with drugs or being alert and alive without them. Drugs rob life of the natural sensations and joy, which are the only reasons for living anyhow.

Kate Ceberano
Ceberano Productions
31 Greville Street
Prahran, Victoria 3181

AUTHOR'S NOTE

I never knew Anna Wood and from all that I have learned about her, that was my loss. Inevitably, writing this book has been a sad experience, even though everyone concerned has managed to share a great deal of warmth and even a laugh or two along the way.

I agreed to write *Anna's Story* for two reasons. First, Jennie Orchard, at HarperCollins, asked me to . . . and although it was an invitation to months of anguish, it was a challenge too important to refuse. This book was Jennie's idea and without her enthusiasm and encouragement it would never have happened.

The second reason was because I, too, have adolescent children and while I can only imagine the sorrow of Anna's parents, I would like to think that this book might, somehow, in some way, prevent their tragedy from being repeated too many times.

I make no apology for referring to teenagers, children and adolescents as "kids". It's what we call them. It's what they call themselves. I wish there was a better word that included both girls and boys, but there is not.

Because there will always be life after books, Anna Wood's friends were all invited to use pseudonyms when telling their stories. I have indicated those who did with an asterisk at their first mention in the text.

I would like to thank Dr David Bennett, Mr John Malouf, Mr Paul Dillon, Dr Simon Clarke, Mr Athol Moffitt, Dr Peta Odgers, Mr Chris Thomas, Detective Senior Constable Steven Page and Dr Malcolm Parmenter for their invaluable help with my research. I am indebted to the Centre for Education and Information on Drugs and Alcohol (CEIDA) for much of the information on drugs and drug use. I would also like to express my appreciation to the Australian Medical Association for their support.

I want to thank my family for caring so much, in particular my own daughter Anna, who provided an invaluable teenage perspective as well as unlimited tea and sympathy.

Finally, I thank Angela and Tony Wood, whose sincerity, courage and compassion is an inspiration to parents everywhere. Whatever happens now, Angie and Tony, her sweetness and light will not be forgotten.

Bronwyn Donaghy
1996

PROLOGUE

In December 1995, in a school hall strung with streamers, eighty children gathered with their teachers to celebrate the end of their seven years of primary school.

It was a sultry summer evening; they had spent the day making wall hangings – gigantic cutouts of jungle animals, luridly coloured – and looping cascades of crepe paper from the beams in the ceiling.

They now wore their best clothes, the girls in short, flared dresses and sly little sandals, the boys in baggy jeans, flowing shirts and enormous shoes, every inch of their burgeoning puberty hidden from view. Hair – braided, under-cut, moulded and moussed – shone. Cheeks glowed.

The hall was full of talk and laughter. They'd groomed themselves and preened for the cameras – the dressed, the pressed and the odd catastrophe. They'd feasted on fast food and listened to a speech or two.

Now it was time to dance.

A teacher who had complimented the children by also turning up in her Sunday best, pressed the button on the giant ghetto-blaster and as tortured piano notes trembled in the hall, the boys chose their partners for the Pride of Erin.

They'd been practising for weeks. They had learned to step and slide, to dip and kick, to go forward and back and side-together-side. They whirled, they twirled, they clung, they flung, they counted and they kept in time. Most of the time.

The barn dance followed; the girls chose their partners for the gypsy tap and then, daringly, they all attempted the samba. They swivelled their skinny hips, pointed their booted toes, wriggled their hands and passed on their partners. A very plump boy sweated profusely as his lips moved in time with the beat;

his very plump partner beamed from one end of her lovely face to the other. A kid with a fringe of black satin hair whirled his exquisite almond-eyed girl around the floor as if he was a bullfighter and she was his cape.

The others smiled and counted.

When the music stopped they cheered; they clapped their hands and called for more.

Most of them were twelve years old. In a few weeks' time they would be starting high school. Big-time. Teenagers. Growing up. Growing tall. Growing smarter. Doing different things. Making choices.

In a few months' time it would take more than music and laughter and friendship to make them happy.

Right now they were still kids, counting and smiling in their smart clean clothes.

PART ONE

....

THE LOOKING GLASS

In fancy they pursue
The dream-child moving through a land
Of wonders wild and new . . .
(*Alice in Wonderland*, Lewis Carroll)

Above: *Anna (right) with her sister, Alice, April 1981.*
Below left: *Ready to start school, 1985.*
Below right: *Anna with her father, Tony, 1992.*

INTRODUCTION

The spring of 1995 never really grew up. Born out of a bleak and whingeing winter, it slipped into the extremes of adolescence and stayed there, sullen and cold one day, sparkling with promise the next.

It was a teenage spring, moody and unpredictable. Some days were energetic and vital, windswept, shining and clear. Others were tremulous and tearful, with too much rain and freezing nights that made people long for the childish comforts of winter which had by then been put away.

Its belligerence was hard to tolerate. Dangerous and stormy, impatient, stubborn and unreliable, one week spring was determined to hang back, sulking in the cold and wet, days later it was glowing with delight, embracing everyone in irresistible warmth, light-hearted, lovely and silly with sunshine.

The people began longing for summer. Worn out with the moods of spring, they yearned for consistency and calm, for the maturity and peace that warm wise days might bring.

1

ANGELA'S STORY

It was peaches that brought Angela Brown to Australia. She was drawn by the sun and the sea but especially by the soft golden fruit from which dream desserts were made. In Accrington, a working-class town in the north of England, known only for its defunct football team and its bricks, thirteen-year-old Angela learned all about the fruit-growing regions of Australia and decided any place where peaches came from would be close to heaven.

"They were canned peaches I was dreaming about," she smiled, twenty years later. "It wasn't the freshness that counted. It was just the thought of all that luscious fruit, sliced and packed into tins, that sent my imagination into a spin."

When Angela left school, she saved her wages from office and hotel work and set out for Melbourne in 1974. A few months later she moved to Sydney and met Tony.

She was a tall, cool English girl with a strong, smooth face, luminous skin, a wicked sense of humour and the same lovely smile which would be inherited by her daughters. He was a frank and friendly Australian, with a lively grin and laughing eyes; he was earnest, honest and lots of fun. You could almost say they went together like peaches and cream.

They met in a bar ("I'm afraid to say"), in Brookvale, in June 1974. Tony was with a mate and claimed it was his first night out as a free man after the failure of his first marriage. He and Angela

4

began going out together about six months later. They were friends, she said, before they were ever lovers. They were married in December 1976 and he is still the best friend she has.

Angela was thrilled when she discovered she was pregnant with Alice. She was twenty-nine and her biological clock was sounding the alarm – she immediately planned a second baby within two years. Anna came a little earlier than she expected, which was even better.

"We were living in southern Queensland and Tony and I had taken Alice with us to the Indooroopilly Shopping Centre. I said to Tony: 'You know, I think I'm pregnant again. I'm going to see.' I went into one of those chemist shops where you can get a quick test done and half an hour later I went back. The result was positive. I remember thinking, 'Oh fantastic' – I was so happy. Tony and Alice were waiting outside in the car. I raced over to them, so excited and said: 'Yes, yes, we're having another baby!' We were both absolutely over the moon."

Anna Victoria Wood was born on 27 May 1980 in Southport, Queensland, the Gold Coast's only truly serious suburb. It was an easy birth; she suckled happily at her mother's breast and slept peacefully a few minutes after her arrival in the world. Angela and Anna spent a few days together in hospital and then Tony and Alice came to escort Anna to the first of what would be many places she would call home.

Angela wrote in her diary: "It is lovely to be home again. Alice seems so big after spending so much time with Anna. Anna has darker hair than her sister and the cutest little face."

Tony Wood had built a cool and spacious bungalow at Nerang for his small family and was running a very successful business with his new concrete truck. Angela had two gorgeous daughters, a circle of good friends and she still looked stunning in a yellow bikini; they were all blissfully happy.

"With a two-and-a-half-year-old and a new baby," wrote Angela in her diary, "time seems to race away and our daily routine seems very haphazard. However, we do manage to fit in many cuddles between feeding, sleeping and washing! Anna isn't quite the addicted sucker that Alice was – she seems to know when she has had enough. She is a strong child and at four weeks is desperately trying to pull herself up into sitting position. She is gaining weight steadily, even with a cold – a very cuddly and adorable little girl.

"Tony and I can't believe our good fortune at having two gorgeous girls. Tony does his share of patting and rocking and it's a lovely sight, little Anna thrown over her daddy's shoulder, fast asleep."

When Anna was three months old the Woods returned to Sydney and bought a delicatessen business in the beachside suburb of Manly, moving into a house at Little Manly Beach. Anna seemed to thrive on the long journeys involved in the move, and remained in good humour despite the interruptions to her routine.

"She is such a happy girl, always a smile! Daddy says she will get a sore face if she keeps it up . . . Tony's voice is the cue for grins and gurgles, an instant reaction!"

Not long after they moved, Tony became ill. Angela took his place at the shop and, while he convalesced, Tony spent several weeks as a house-husband. "He loved it," said Angela. "The washing, the ironing, the cooking – he didn't mind because it meant he could be with the girls.

"He has always shared them in every way. If they woke in the night, he would get them and bring them to me. It was never a bone of contention – he never said: 'It's your turn.'"

By the time Anna started walking, at thirteen months, she was also asking questions. Her favourite expression, which she applied to everyone and everything was: "What's that?"

She was extraordinarily affectionate and, according to her mother's diary, "can't get enough touching, kissing and cuddling." She also had a bad temper. "She is easily aroused and is not afraid to shout when things aren't going her way."

She wasn't at all happy about being weaned at fifteen months. "She pulls at my buttons," wrote Angela, "looks dolefully into my eyes and asks for 'tip' – who could refuse? I hate refusing her when it is obvious she wants the comfort of sucking rather than the nourishment. We try and give more cuddles to compensate but somehow I think she'd prefer the real thing."

Anna would never stay in her own bed. "The first two or three weeks after we brought her home from hospital she had a good sleeping pattern," said Angela. "But once she got a taste for our bed, that was it. She was still coming into bed with us when she was eight. She wouldn't wake you. You would just become aware of this presence at your side and then she would snuggle in.

"Initially we just had a mattress on the floor and she was always there, in the middle."

Anna, said her mother, was always the sort of child you wanted to kiss. "Unlike Alice, she liked to be touched and cuddled. She loved the soft part of my upper arm – she liked to hold it while she suckled. When she learned to talk, she would call it 'belbow'.

"'Ooh, belbow, belbow,' she'd say, and she'd put her hand up my sleeve and a look of contentment would slide across her face.

"She has always stayed a very tactile person. She had a hug and a kiss for everyone."

When Anna was eighteen months old her mother again made a note of her lightning flashes of rage. "She loses her temper easily but fortunately calms as quickly as she flares up. She is almost always happy and agreeable. She and Alice get on quite well – I hope it lasts."

It didn't. A year later her mother noted in her diary that when the girls fought, skin and hair flew everywhere! "Anna has a very determined nature," wrote Angela, "and is quite adamant when she feels disinclined to do whatever is required of her. It's a battle of wills! She has developed a wonderful vocabulary of swearwords which she uses when necessary – which is often!"

When Anna started preschool kindergarten, aged three, she set a precedent for life. She found a "best friend" who needed her – a little girl with a speech problem. "Anna shows a protective instinct towards those not quite so capable of standing up for themselves," wrote Angela. It was an aspect of Anna's character which would become stronger as she grew older. "She can be very vocal if she feels there is unfairness afoot. Anna has always had a very loud voice which she uses to her advantage."

In 1983, the family moved to Davidson, a leafy residential suburb near Sydney's northern beaches and an area which was attracting young families because of its proximity to both sea and bush. New schools, wide roads and modern amenities were being established. It seemed an ideal place for the Wood girls to grow up.

Anna started school in a little green uniform at the age of four and three-quarters. She made another "best friend" and it became obvious that she was a left-hander. "She has no difficulty with the alphabet and colours," noted her mother, "but she tends to write back to front."

A year later Angela made another entry about her daughter's character, which remained accurate a decade later. "Anna is very self-assured now and not afraid to speak out. She has lots of confidence and, what's more, has a wonderful, happy, loving and giving nature. Anna would give her arm away if she thought someone needed it enough.

"She is extremely thoughtful where others are concerned, can turn to tears at the sight of baby animals and that sort of thing, but is shrewd enough to know when advantage is being taken of her."

Tony and Angela decided to invest in a coffee-importing business and eventually sold their delicatessen. Angela only worked when the children were at school. In 1986 the family moved to the Central Coast and Tony became a commuter; Anna swapped her little green uniform for a little red one and, to use her new teacher's words, "settled in like silk" on her very first day of school.

Anna was a mischievous child but everyone found it difficult to be angry with her. "I would have to bite inside my cheek to stop laughing when I was chastising her," admitted Angela. "She wasn't naughty, but she was full of fun and very inquisitive. 'Why' and 'how' were her favourite words.

"You couldn't just show her something, and say 'Look'. You couldn't say 'Don't touch'. She had to feel it, try it, hold it, know more about it than you could tell her.

"You couldn't just give her a simple explanation. She'd say: 'But why?' You couldn't palm her off with excuses. She would want to know why, when, what it was, what it felt like, what it was made of, where, how, what would happen? If you were talking to Anna you couldn't end a sentence. Even when she was finished with you, she wouldn't take your word for anything. She always had to find out for herself."

Another year passed and Angela and Tony decided to try their fortune in England. They packed up their small family and spent three months in South Yorkshire, while they looked about for a suitable business. Anna and Alice were enrolled at the local school and Anna acquired yet another "best friend" – a little girl who looked so much like Anna that they swapped coats and bags to confuse their mothers. It almost always worked!

The Woods bought a pub in Warwick-on-Eden, in Cumbria, and spent the first two years living "over the shop". While their parents ran *The Queen's Arms*, the two girls went to a nearby school where, once again, Anna acquired a host of friends. Deciding that family life was suffering because of the long hours they spent working in the pub restaurant and behind the bar, Angela and Tony moved the family into a flat behind the pub, where Angela at least was able to organise more time with the children.

"I missed so much in the first two years of living over the pub," said Angela. "I realised Anna had a brilliant sense of humour; she was a good mimic, full of fun, a laugh a minute – until things weren't going her way. Then tempers would flare and things would fly! Her anger never lasted for long. Suddenly it would be 'Sorry, Mum' and big hugs and kisses."

Anna and Alice – who later went to a nearby boarding school – grew up in the boisterous bustle of pub life, where their pretty faces and their beaming smiles made them favourites among the local people. There were nights of laughter and singing, there was snow, there were seasons out of story books, theme parties, silly hats, bike rides on icy roads and long, brisk walks through the countryside. They had anoraks instead of parkas, grass instead of lawn, gardens instead of yards. There were insipid summers, exquisite springs, bad winters and good friends.

"They were happy years," said Angela. "We had so many friends and because we lived so close by, we were both always there for the girls. We had a wonderful time, although it was very hard work and long hours."

During her childhood in two hemispheres Anna was never seriously ill – she lived on both sides of the world without ever suffering more than an occasional wheeze and a runny nose. She had measles at eighteen months, chicken pox at two-and-a-half and mild exercise-induced asthma at twelve. Anna never had a serious disease, she never broke any bones or had an operation. She was in hospital only twice in her life – at the very beginning and at the very end.

She was a good swimmer who took Ventolin to ease the occasional tightness in her chest brought on during intermittent training sessions at the local pool. She needed no other medication.

After four years the Wood family returned to Australia. The reason, said Angela, was simple. It was Tony's home and he missed it.

"We came back here, to Belrose. We were familiar with the northern beaches, we felt it was a good place for the girls to go to school. We bought a takeaway food business. But we had been away for a long time and we were very out of touch with what was going on here. We began losing money.

"I rang the people I had done some work for in earlier years and they offered me a job. I went back to work in the drama department of a company which publishes educational material.

"Tony tried to make the business work for the next few years but eventually it failed. We lost everything. Tony is now a contractor with an insurance company. We're trying to build up our lives again. We live in a rented house. But we're coping. We have each other."

While their business was struggling, more trouble stirred. From out of the past, a small, simmering secret bubbled up and overflowed.

Anna, the smiling golden girl upon whom Nature seemed to have bestowed more than her share of blessings, the child who had always been so generous with her affection, confided to her sister that she had a problem.

The onset of puberty had opened a window in Anna's mind that had remained closed since she was three. At the age of twelve she began having disturbing memories of being sexually molested over a period of months by an older child. The girl, who would have been about twelve at the time, was the daughter of some former acquaintances.

"I didn't know what to do about it," said Angela. "I tried to talk to Anna about what had happened. I explained to her that she was a victim, that what had happened to her was a violation of her human rights. But she found it very difficult to talk about, even to me. 'That's enough,' she'd say. 'It's enough.'

"She felt guilty. She said thinking about it made her feel bad.

"The girl is a woman now and we wanted to confront her, to bring it out into the open. Anna refused. I am very concerned even now that Anna did not want anyone talking publicly about it.

"It's just that it might provide a key to the way Anna felt about herself.

"I arranged for Anna to have counselling. She saw a psychologist for about six months and then she became tired of it and asked if she could stop. I don't think any of it made Anna feel any better about herself."

Anna, being Anna, bounced back. When she was thirteen, an English teacher at her school asked if she was interested in being a props assistant for a production of *Little Shop of Horrors*, which was being produced by the Forest Youth Theatre. "Anna was organised and good at the job and she liked the people," said Angela. "I became involved in it as well. It was a welcome break from the pressure of the financial problems we were wrestling with at the time.

"When they decided to do *The Mikado*, Anna was in the chorus and Alice joined as well. Then they were both in *Grease*. They loved it – we all did.

"Anna also loved reading and all sorts of music. She learned flute for a year when she was in Year Seven at high school. But Anna was a dabbler. She threw herself into life with enthusiasm but she made no long-term commitment to sport or music. For the past year she's been passionate about techno music. It was the sort of music her group preferred.

"Another bad thing that happened around that time," said Angela, "was that one night Tony and I had a terrible row. Our life has had its peaks and its troughs and a lot of it has been very tough. Financial pressures cause many problems with families and we were no exception.

"However, we had never done much arguing and certainly not in front of the children. On this night, we did and Anna was there. Alice was away on holiday. We were at the dinner table, just the three of us.

"There was a lot of pressure on Tony all through 1994 when the business was going downhill. He was desperately worried about what was happening. The fact that I was working didn't help him. He is a real Aussie battler – it is important to him to be the breadwinner for the family.

"I know I never seemed to be at home – I was always at the office and then I started spending my spare time working with the theatre group. That night, I said something that just made Tony snap and then it was all on. We said some terrible things to each other.

"Anna was very upset. She left the table in tears. I went upstairs to see if she was okay; I told her everything would be all right, that married couples had rows, that it was normal.

"I don't think she really forgave us for a long time. She was very confused about it. Sometimes I wonder if we should have fought in front of them more than we did. I don't know if she ever understood that despite the troubles we have been through together over the years, or perhaps because of them, one of the most important priorities in my life is for Tony to be happy."

Anna had always been more interested in making friends than in setting academic records. "She was at school," said Angela, "primarily for the social life."

Despite early indications of a bright and questioning mind, Anna was an average student. She did her homework in the playground before school and her assignments on the day before they were due in. Her diary and essays contain flashes of giftedness; the depth of some of her poetry obviously shocked and surprised the teachers who read them.

But not surprisingly, she was often told by her teachers that while she had enormous potential to do well, she needed to try much harder.

She always had good intentions. In Year Ten she made a contract with herself and asked her mother to witness it:

I, Anna Wood, have decided to try the best I can in school. I am going to whip the pants off a lot of good students in school. Not one piece of homework will be late and not one assignment will be not finished. I am going to do my Best. Signed: Anna Wood.

From the beginning, Anna and her sister, Alice, were very different. Alice, the older daughter, was always a clear thinker, very organised, exceptionally honest and much more reserved than her little sister.

Anna on the other hand was volatile and highly emotional.

"She was a crusader," said Angela. "She always wanted to get involved. She loved people. She fidgeted, she could never sit still, she was excitable – she was the ultimate chatterbox.

"Her philosophy seemed to be: 'Why use one word when you can use twelve?' The only time she was still was when she was asleep."

Being so unalike, Alice and Anna quarrelled a lot. "Anna had enormous regard for her sister, but she'd say 'Alice is so stuck-up.' It was largely because Alice would only speak if she had something to say. Anna would talk about anything – or nothing.

"Anna was an extremely likeable person but in the last year she became more outspoken. She was more sure of what she was talking about and not at all backward about coming forward with her views. She had very strong opinions about people's behaviour and she didn't mind telling them.

"She told people who took drugs they were fools."

"Every night at the dinner table, we talked openly to our girls about everything under the sun, including the problems that face today's families.

"When our business was in trouble, Tony and I talked about our financial problems in front of them. We discussed so many issues – sex, contraception, AIDS, drugs, all those things that worry parents today. It was never a problem communicating with Anna. She had an opinion on everything. She was an all-or-nothing person – halfway was never good enough for her.

"A friend once said how much she envied our relationship with our girls. 'You and Tony communicate so openly with Alice and Anna,' she said. 'You talk to each other all the time.' I thought she was right. But whatever we said was obviously not enough.

"We talked about sexual matters more than the drug problem. I think you do, particularly when you have daughters. In my day, sex was the big taboo.

"Anna was worried about not developing as fast as many of her friends. She didn't begin menstruating until she was thirteen and three months. We discussed virginity. I told her that a sexual act with another person was a very special thing, something you didn't do without giving it a great deal of thought. Anna said: 'Mum, I couldn't even think about doing that with a boy . . . I'd have to really really love him and there isn't anybody like that in my life.' She was fourteen and a half at the time and her attitude to sex may have changed in the last six months. She was growing up fast and her body was changing, although she was still very moral when it came to flesh showing or anything like that. I think she was still a virgin. If she hadn't been, I feel she would have told me about it.

"You can't be alive today and not know there is a problem with drugs in our community," said Angela. "There are serious problems with legal drugs, like alcohol and cigarettes, and illegal ones, like marijuana, LSD and the new designer drugs they are bringing into the country.

"Like most parents, I talked to my girls about the temptation of drugs. I did it from a sense of duty, without ever considering that it was something that would really affect anyone in our family.

"We had our first serious discussion about mind-altering drugs when Anna was twelve or thirteen. We talked about the problem as if it was something that only happened to other people's children.

"I'm so ashamed when I think about it now.

"I gave them as much information as I had, but that wasn't a lot. The message I tried to get across was that people who take drugs behave in an erratic way. It was – it still is – what worries me most. That our children could be with people who are out of control.

"I said to Anna one night: 'I couldn't bear for anything to happen to you, if you were with someone who was drunk or took drugs.'

"She replied: 'Mum, do you think I'm stupid?'"

Anna was not secretive. She never closed her bedroom door. But she told little lies to keep out of trouble. She lied about why she hadn't eaten her school lunches. She lied about the phone. She knew how to make it ring; she would then hold down the button and dial her friends' numbers so that her parents thought she was taking an incoming call. They were little lies, the sort of fibs that are accepted by nineties parents as being part of the adolescent phenomenon.

She didn't lie about trying cigarettes – she just didn't mention it. Her mother almost laughed at her.

"I can smell it on your clothes, Anna," said Angela.

But Anna refused to be drawn into an argument about smoking. She never wanted rows with her parents.

"She wasn't ever rude or horrible. She slammed a lot of doors. That's about as far as she ever went."

As Angela and Tony only suspected that Anna smoked, they turned a blind eye, accepting it as a minor act of revolt and an inevitable part of growing up.

"The main people in Anna's life were her schoolfriends," said Angela. "Most of them were really lovely young people, both boys and girls.

"When she went to The Forest High she became friends with a lovely girl named Eddie and they were very close, even spending holidays together, until Eddie's parents decided to send her to a different school.

"Anna also had a friend called Sarine, an Armenian girl with very strict parents, who also invited Anna to stay at home a great deal. Sarine was part of Anna's group at school and she became very close to us as well.

"I was less certain about some of the others.

"Anna had always been attracted to underdogs, to people who needed her friendship because they had problems. Some of the other girls in the group had troubled lives – split families, that sort of thing. Anna would stay at their houses overnight and they would come and stay here, but Tony and I were worried. We had certain rules when the girls were here – rules about swearing, smoking, respect for other people in the house – and we always made sure we were around.

"We weren't sure if the same no-nos existed in all the other girls' houses.

"In the last two months of Anna's life, I don't know if our rules had any effect on Anna at all. I was very busy at work. I was there for long hours. Tony travelled a lot that year. He went away to work for several weeks at a time and although he phoned frequently I knew she was missing him very much.

"Tony and Anna were very close. I loved to see them together. I thought it was wonderful that Anna wasn't rejecting us the way many children do when they reach adolescence.

"When he was away last year, she started coming into my bed again, just as she did when she was a little girl."

Angela Wood is still a handsome woman. She dresses with casual style and has a fabulous figure for a woman of forty-eight – of course, she's a lot thinner than she was a few months ago. When Tony is away working, she often forgets to eat. She moves around the house with restless energy but when she stops to talk about her daughter, she sits very still.

Her hair is silky and stick-straight, just like Anna's. Her face is strong-boned, smooth-planed, and although she smiles Anna's smile, the grief there is so raw that sometimes – often – it's kinder to look away.

"I have been working full-time since 1991. I used to drive Alice, Anna and her friend Chloe* to school every morning. Chloe lives just around the corner in the next street. I would drop them at the shopping centre.

"Anna and Alice were in the habit of ringing me at work when they got home from school, to tell me what they were going to do during the afternoon. Anna rang me every day. She'd say: 'I'm going over to Chloe's' or 'I need a lift to Alexia's*'. When Tony wasn't away on business he would usually get home before me and he would drive her to her friends' houses.

"Sometimes she would ask to do something that we felt was unwise. We'd say: 'That's not on. We would worry about you going to something like that.' She never made a fuss.

"The biggest issue was when she wanted to go to a rave party to celebrate her fifteenth birthday in May 1995. Her friends had offered to buy her a ticket. 'You dance all night,' she told me, 'and you don't come home until the morning.' I asked her where this party would be. 'You don't know where until the day,' she said. 'It's part of the fun. Then they advertise it at the last minute.'

"That day I asked a young man at work about rave parties. He told me there were lots of drugs at them, so I went home and told Anna there was no way her father would give his permission for her to be at a place like that.

"I told her if she still wanted to go she would have to lie to her father about where she was.

"She went to school and thought about it. She rang me that afternoon and said: 'I'm not going. I'm not going to lie to Dad.'

* indicates pseudonym

"Sometime between May and October she was prepared to start lying.

"When she started talking about an older boy called George*, I was worried. I wondered why a nineteen-year-old would want to hang around with fifteen-year-old girls. But then she bought him home for dinner and I was charmed. He was just a little guy, not sophisticated or loud. He was gentle. I could see why Anna and her friends liked him.

"By the time she turned fifteen, we were becoming more uneasy about some of the people in her group and we started thinking about sending her to another school. It's not that her reports were terrible. It was just obvious that she could have done so much better. She was being distracted by her friends.

"Alice didn't like a couple of Anna's friends at all. She made no secret of it.

"Anna would say to us: 'Why don't you like my friends? What's wrong with them? Why do you like Alice's friends and not mine?'

"All I could say was: 'I just don't think the combination's good.'"

"All her life, Anna's favourite ambition was to make people beautiful.

"When we were in England, a friend of mine who had perfect fingernails tried to talk Anna out of biting hers. She said: 'You are a beautiful girl but you have ugly fingers. If you give up biting your nails I'll give you a manicure at a beauty parlour.'

"Anna grew her nails and my friend did as she promised. When Anna came home from the salon she said: '*That's* what I want to do.' She was seven years old but she never changed her mind.

"We had assumed she would remain at school until she had done her Higher School Certificate at the end of Year Twelve, but one day a friend of Alice's who worked in a beauty salon came over and told us they were looking for a junior apprentice. It seemed like the answer to a lot of Anna's problems. We had been thinking of sending her to a different school, so she could make some new friends, but she wasn't really interested in academic achievement. This would give her a profession.

"Anna gave it a lot of thought. She kept asking us if she was doing the right thing. She started going in on Saturdays, for work experience. Everyone at the salon loved her. Anna had a lovely smile and perfect teeth. I think they liked having her there.

"She left school in October. She had two weeks off and she was due to start full-time work at the beginning of November.

"Looking back, I realise the subject of drugs started coming up more often during Anna's last weeks at school. I still didn't think about drugs being an issue for us, although there was talk . . . One of Anna's friends had been experimenting with drugs. She ran away from home and stayed away for two days. Her father had rung us to see if we knew where she was.

"Anna told me she had lost patience with her. 'She's just not thinking,' she said. 'It's all too much.'

"Perhaps Anna herself dabbled in something. She didn't tell us about it. Apart from anything else, Anna never had any money and you need plenty of cash to buy drugs. She was not a material girl. Money slipped through her fingers like water. Even in the five weeks she had been working Saturdays at the beauty salon, she hadn't managed to save up any money.

"Alice told me the kids at school rave on to each other about how good drugs make you feel – especially the drug called ecstasy. They say it gives you confidence, that it makes you feel as if you can do anything.

"To look at Anna she seemed very confident, but I know her self-esteem wasn't as high as most people who knew her assumed it to be. She had the same doubts and fears about how she looked and how she behaved as any normal young girl going through adolescence. I know it bothered her that she didn't have a steady boyfriend, whereas some of her friends did. Yet just about every boy she knew had a crush on her – they've been telling us ever since.

"I can't believe she felt so badly about herself that she needed drugs to boost her confidence. She was so popular and so pretty.

"Sometimes in the last few months, just looking at Anna almost took my breath away. I watched her loveliness blossom without her even being aware of it.

"She started asking me why I was looking at her. She asked me a lot, in those last weeks, why I looked at her so much. When I told her, she wouldn't believe me.

"She said: 'My Mum's a witch. She can read my mind. She knows what I'm thinking. She knows what I'm going to do.'

"But I didn't."

2

TONY'S STORY

From his firm, dry handshake to his wrinkling, twinkling eyes, his ambling gait and his chipped front tooth, Tony Wood is everyone's favourite image of the Aussie battler. His hair is grizzled, his gaze is direct, his grin is broad. When he says that all he's ever wanted to be is an ordinary bloke and that all he's ever wanted to do is provide for and protect his family, you know he's speaking the truth.

He has been cheated of his most precious reason for living; he is angry, disillusioned and exhausted, but he is neither down nor out. He is up and fighting. He is determined to find out why drugs are so readily available to children in Australia, and to do something about it.

Tony Wood is straight as a slide rule and honest to a fault. It may be a problem for the drug dealers he has taken on. It could turn out to be a problem for Tony as well.

The bitterness of his loss has not diminished the warmth, the generosity nor even the humour of this man. He keeps his sadness locked away. Sometimes when he speaks of her, it seeps into his eyes and he looks lost. Sometimes, just for a while, he can't go on.

"The odd thing is, it turned out that none of us ever thought Anna would grow old. We never discussed it, but at the hospital we all spoke of it for the first time. Angie said Anna was not a long-term child. She had no image of where she would go. I could never imagine Anna growing up and having children of her own. Even Alice said she had always felt something would happen to Anna before she grew old.

"None of us knew why we felt it and none of us ever spoke of it until that weekend. But there was something vulnerable about Anna which we all felt and none of us understood.

"Later we found a letter in which Anna mentioned it too.

"Alice is a different person. She is very down to earth, she isn't vulnerable at all. Alice was born wise. When she popped out of Angie's womb, the first thing she did was to look around at us to make sure we were the right sort of parents for her.

"Anna arrived tired. She wanted to go back to sleep. 'I've done my work for the day,' she seemed to say, 'now I'm sleeping.'

"She used to hang over my shoulder while I worked. She'd sleep all day, like a little koala. She wouldn't go to sleep for anyone except me and if I put her down, she'd wake up.

"My eldest daughter, Glenda, from my first marriage, had arrived very quickly, only a couple of months after the wedding. I was only twenty-three then and still crazy. There should be a law against blokes getting married before they turn thirty.

"When Angie and I got married it was like a big party, with a solemn bit in the middle, under the trees. It was very relaxed. We married because we wanted children.

"Anna was a delight from the start. When she started talking, she had a real wit. Right from the beginning, we had some of our best times around the dinner table. The television would always go off and we always ate together. They knew the rules. Dinner-time was family time.

"We had a very happy family life. I had a lot of joy out of it. An unbelievable amount really. I only wished I had sons when the football was on. No, really, you get what you get. Our girls made us very happy.

"When we came back to Sydney from the Gold Coast and I was sick I spent a lot of time with the girls. Angie went to work in the shop two days a week and I had those days with the kids. I got to know our children really well, something I don't think a lot of fathers really get the chance to do. I'm not a sporting person, so even after I had recovered, I spent all the time I could with my daughters.

"Anna was always attracted to the underdog. Even when we lived on the Central Coast and she was only six years old, she got tangled up with unsuitable kids – kids who weren't like her, who weren't being cared for the way she was, but who wanted to be. She came home once with fifty dollars that some child had given her. She gave it to me. She didn't know why they'd given it to her and she wasn't interested.

"The biggest upset about Anna that I can remember was when we were in England and I was really busy in the pub. I was running my backside off. Anna hurt herself and I couldn't do anything about it, I couldn't cuddle her. I thought: 'This isn't right.' The next day I felt sad about it. I believed that if you were in a service industry, you had to provide top service.

"But I was angry with myself that I hadn't put my little girl first."

"I don't remember ever getting cranky with Anna herself. She had such a way with her that if she did something naughty and you were trying to chastise her, you'd be grinning and laughing at her instead.

"She'd get cranky with *you*. She'd charge up the stairs, swinging away, slamming doors. Then she'd be down again ten minutes later apologising.

"Anna was a little terror to take out. She would mess about all the time – she'd never miss knocking her drink over. I used to take her out and make her sit in the car until she promised to come back and behave herself. She was so clumsy, all arms and legs. So she'd come back in, big smile, 'Sorry Dad, sorry Mum,' and I'd forgive her and buy her a fresh drink – and then she'd knock it over again.

"She used to go ice-skating when she was quite young and she was so brilliant and graceful they told us we should do something to develop her talent. Then she'd come home and fall over a match on the ground. It was amazing.

"I was wondering how tall she was going to be. I wondered whether she would ever grow into her feet. She was tall, she was getting on for about five foot six and I wondered if she was ever going to stop.

"She was only a child to look at. She didn't look eighteen, she didn't go out looking eighteen that last night, she went out looking like a little girl. I don't know how she ever got into that club.

"She acted like a kid. She wouldn't go past you without giving you a hug. She was still just a little girl, really.

"Alice and Anna are two different kids and I was close to them in different ways. When she grew older, Alice used to come in to help me out at work and we would talk for hours. Anna would come in to work to get money but she wasn't very interested in working. She always had too many other things going on with her mates.

"I cuddled Anna more. That was because she was more of a cuddler. Anna and I were very close, closer I think than she was to Angie, because mothers and daughters clash a bit sometimes. She loved us both, but if Angie and I had a bit of an argument, Anna would side with me. If I was away she would ring me up just to say how much she missed me.

"When I'm on the road, working, I miss the sound of her voice so much. 'Hi Dad! How are you doing?' I miss that so much. It's hard to talk about really."

"When we were having problems with the business Angie and I clashed a bit, but we tried not to show it to the girls. I don't know how much Anna knew or worried about our money troubles. If she did, she didn't mention it.

"I didn't realise that Anna was ever unhappy until after she died and I read her letters. She was apparently angry that her mum was working long hours and weekends and I was away a lot in the last three months before she died. I had to go where the work was available. I thought she understood why I had to go away. We needed to build up our bank account again.

"I still don't think it was a serious problem for her.

"A letter came for Anna the other day. It was her bank statement. She had eight dollars in her account.

"Anna had no use for money. She didn't save. When she started working at the beauty salon she earned twenty dollars each Saturday, but it slipped through her fingers like water. She spent anything she had on her friends. She didn't get pocket money, but I would give her something to spend when she went out. If I gave her ten dollars, she would never bring any of it home. She'd buy everyone McDonald's. She'd shout them whatever they wanted.

"It wasn't that she needed money to make her popular. Anna was an incredible kid, she really was. She made everyone feel special. She treated everybody the same, whether they were boys or girls.

"The older she got, the more she worried about her friends. She was a giver. She spent all her time on the people around her. She talked for hours to the school counsellor – but never about herself, only about all these other kids.

"Anna was no angel. I've seen her have a quick smoke and a swig of beer when she thought I wasn't looking. I'm not going to crucify her for that – what kid hasn't done that when they're growing up?

"I thought the crowd she was hanging around with were no-hopers. I wanted to tell her they were like leeches, hanging off her, clinging to the goodness that was in her. I hated the way they talked, the slang they used. She couldn't even sit at the dinner table with us for five minutes without one of them ringing her.

"I wanted to tell her how I felt about those friends of hers but Angie wouldn't let me. She said Anna had the right to choose her own friends.

"I don't know what you do about a problem like that. You can't choose their friends for them and you can't tell your kids they can't go out, not when they get older. So what can you do?

"She knew in her own mind how we felt because we had discussed sending her to a different school. If she hadn't got that job, we would have insisted on that. But she said to me: 'You know, Dad, they are the best friends I've ever had, those people.'"

"We were still doing most of our talking around the dinner table. We always ate together and talked. Even though the girls were growing up, the rules didn't change. We talked about everything, including drugs. Anna told us about a girl she knew whose parents were addicts; she was very concerned for that girl.

"It's so hard to believe that you can have all the right rules in the world and talk to your children about everything and your kid can still die.

"After we lost Anna I had the opportunity of seeing some correspondence between her and another girl who had a serious problem with drugs. We knew this girl's family and we knew about her problem. Anna had been worried about her and she had talked about her to us. The girl's father showed me the letters Anna and her friends had written to his daughter.

"It was interesting that when the others wrote to this girl they talked a lot about drugs and they used very coarse language. I was distraught after reading what they said and I came home and went up to Anna's room and went through her own letters for the first time. She had letters from her friends, too. But her mail was entirely different. When they wrote to Anna they didn't mention drugs. They wrote an entirely different sort of letter. In all the letters, I found only one mention of drugs.

"Angie feels now that Anna may have experimented a bit before she died. I don't know if it's true. We never saw any evidence of it.

"Anna could have popped that pill, just as the others did, without anything terrible happening to her, and we might never have known anything about it. Or she might have popped it and been a bit sick and decided never to take drugs again.

"If that had happened, I don't think we would have punished her. I can't remember ever punishing Anna, really. Having her stomach pumped or going on oxygen or whatever would have been needed to make her better – quite honestly, that would have been punishment enough.

"I find it very hard to forgive the people who were with Anna that night, not for what they did, but for what they didn't do. If Anna had been taken to hospital six hours earlier, when she first became ill, she might still be with us.

"Anna's living on in four other people now and they are really lucky. She has always been a giver. She has given them her heart, her lungs, her spleen, liver and kidneys and they are very fortunate that our little girl has helped them to live.

"In the end I think Anna went to this death dance they call a rave and tried drugs because so many of the people she knew

29

told her how good it felt. That's all those friends of hers ever talked about and she wouldn't have been able to talk about it too unless she took it as well. That's how I imagine it happened. I can only imagine, because I wasn't there.

"She took that pill and she died.

"I've lost my best mate."

3

ALICE'S STORY

Alice Wood is a serious young person. Her beautiful face, smooth-skinned, framed by a curtain of brown silk hair, looks almost stern in repose. But while Alice's sense of fun surfaces less often than her sister's used to do, her smile transforms her face and her husky laugh is hearty.

Many people regard Alice as an enigma. She has assumed a very public profile since the death of her sister, appearing with media personalities on television, giving interviews, running a youth forum, participating in media stunts and working with the Australian Medical Association to publicise the effects of teenage drug abuse.

They could have forgiven her if she had broken down but through it all the immaculately groomed and beautifully dressed eighteen-year-old remained confident, articulate and composed. Frequently she bestowed on her audiences the exquisite smile of the Wood women.

At home, speaking of her sister, Alice smiled again at the happiest memories. When they ran out she continued to talk, doggedly relating the facts of her sister's short life while tears ran in an unchecked stream down her cheeks.

"My earliest memory of Anna is at Manly. Anna was very little, I can remember Mum pushing her in the pram. I remember feeling jealous when I first saw Anna but not for long. Very soon she was just a part of my family and we all spent time together, playing with her and laughing at the cute things she did. I used to like holding her and helping Mum bath her.

"As we grew older, Anna and I fought like cat and dog and some of my strongest memories are of our arguments. It's funny. They are my fondest memories as well as all the good times we enjoyed together.

"When we were young we went on a lot of long journeys in the car and we would sing together for hours. We knew every word of every song on every Beatles album and we loved singing Abba. Then something would happen, something quite silly, like she would move her leg onto my side, and then we would hit and kick and have an enormous fight. Five minutes later we would have forgotten about it.

"Some of our happiest times together were when we were 'pub kids' in England. That's what everyone called us and all our friends wanted to come and visit because they thought our life was so much more interesting than normal. We would take them around all the rooms when the pub was closed, and we would play restaurants. We'd fill the little liqueur glasses with apple cider and pretend to serve meals.

"Some nights, Anna and I had pub dinners – we were allowed to order anything we wanted from the chef – and we'd sit in the lounge bar and eat our meal and then we'd sing for anyone who would listen. Our favourite act was *Patricia the Stripper*; I would be the narrator and Anna was the stripper. We'd really ham it up, swinging the clothes and tossing the hair, and everybody used to laugh. Even years later, when Mum and Dad had friends over, they'd say: 'Go on, do *Patricia the Stripper*.'

"In England it was so cold at Christmas time, and you'd have a raging fire and everybody would snuggle up together inside. But then it usually got so hot that you were dying to open a window, only you couldn't because the wind was freezing. I remember one Christmas especially. Dad always opened the bar for two hours at lunchtime on Christmas Day; it was his way of saying thank you to his regulars and he often ended up paying for most of the drinks anyway. After they had all left to go home to their own Christmas dinners we always had ours, usually prepared by both Mum and Dad. This time we also invited two of their very best friends.

"Dad served French champagne so there were ice buckets around the place . . . I can't remember how it started but Anna and I began throwing the ice cubes around. Dad said: 'Oy!' but then he joined in and in the end we had the most amazing fight. It was so much fun, we were hysterical. Anna and I ended up in the toilets, hiding behind the door to escape, but Dad stood on a stool and tipped the whole bucket over us. We had the best time, even though we were rather wet. Mum and Dad and their friends and Anna and I laughed so much we all thought we were going to burst.

"On New Year's Eve all the other 'pub kids' – the children of regulars – would come and sleep over with their families. All us kids would have this huge room which was full of all sorts and sizes of beds. It had a balcony which we weren't supposed to go out on, but of course we did. We'd go out there in our pyjamas and there would be snow on the roof and we'd build snowmen until we were blue with cold. It was fabulous!

"I went to boarding school when I was eleven and Anna was like an only child. She used to tell me that she loved it when I went away, but Mum has since told me that Anna hated it. She found it hard to sleep alone in our bedroom when I wasn't there. Mum often had to stay with her until she fell asleep. We always had trouble getting Anna to sleep – right from when she was a little baby.

"We were always performing, but we weren't fussy about an audience. Sometimes we didn't have an audience at all, but we didn't care. We would sing hymns if we ran out of other songs; we found them in our school hymn book, called *Songs of Praise*. We'd sing them at home and in the car – all the time. Anna loved music. Her favourite CD was *Phantom of the Opera*.

"We loved dressing up. We made heaps of home videos, but we never kept them.

"She didn't want to come back to Australia because, being Anna, she had so many friends over there. But of course she came here and made heaps more friends and became a real 'Aussie chick'.

"When we first came back to Australia from England, Mum and Dad were thinking of settling in South Australia, so we drove from Sydney to Adelaide. So we got in the car and two days later we arrived! We just couldn't believe it. We couldn't believe that you could drive for two days before reaching the sea. That's how 'English' we had become.

"We were *so* bored on the way. We sang and sang, and we played 'I Spy' and made plans for our new life. On the way we went through a car-wash and Dad said 'Car-washes are so cheap over here' so we spent hours planning how we would set up our own car-washing business and how we would run it. We kept arguing about how much we ought to charge. Anna thought five dollars was far too much!

"Our last fight was when Anna and Kristina were playing Twister in the living room and Anna asked me to spin the wheel for them, because they were all tangled up on the Twister mat.

"I said I would, but I couldn't be bothered doing it properly. I just made something up, like 'right foot on green'. Anna lost her temper and said: 'Alice, you are *so* lazy,' and I told her I wasn't a kid any more, wanting to play silly games. Kristina is our niece. She and Anna always had fun together. They loved each other so much. Whenever Kristina came to our house she would hold onto Anna and follow her like a shadow.

"A lot of people felt that way about Anna."

"Anna was never rude or uncooperative. She really respected Mum and Dad, to the point where she wouldn't do something they didn't like. She wagged school once and she felt so guilty about it that she rang Mum up at work the same day and said: 'Mum, I've done something really bad.'

"She wasn't a good liar.

"I knew Anna smoked cigarettes, but it wasn't a big deal for either of us. I was a social smoker myself. Anna and her friends would have a cigarette out on the verandah. I think Anna started smoking more heavily in the last few months of her life because of the people she mixed with.

"Mum and Dad knew Anna smoked and of course they didn't approve, but they knew there was little they could do when they weren't around.

"Then Anna decided to give up smoking because she was working at the beauty salon. 'You can't work at a lovely place like this and *smoke*,' she said, so she and her friends bought one last packet before giving up, so they said, *forever*.

"I know she has tried marijuana because actually we tried it together. The people around us were doing it and I knew that Anna wanted to try it. All her friends had done it before and she felt as though she was the only one who hadn't. We were spending a lot of time together at that stage, with the theatre group, and she talked about it quite a bit. I felt responsible and wanted to make sure that nothing happened to her when she eventually did try, because I knew that one day she would, whether I was there or not. I thought if I was with her I could make sure she didn't run off or do anything silly while she was on it.

"We got some from one of the boys in our crowd and we tried it at his house. It was a fairly normal thing to do, for kids our age, but I didn't really want to get involved with marijuana. It was a big step for me. But then I thought I'd probably do it at some stage, so I might as well get it over.

"Some people are saying now that Anna was a regular drug user but that isn't true. These rumours have been started by people who may benefit from the lies. They want to believe nothing can happen to them. They say: 'Oh, that only happens to regular users and I only do drugs at weekends,' or something like that. They think that makes it okay.

"Because Anna hung around with kids who did drugs, she ran the risk of getting that reputation.

"I didn't like most of Anna's girlfriends, for the simple reason that I didn't think they were good enough for her. I thought that most of them were dumb and selfish and it ended up that I was right.

"In the last few months of her life, Anna became particularly friendly with George. I knew his sister and I liked her but I was completely wrong about him. I had no idea George was into drugs, and that he was a raver.

"One night she brought this guy around to have dinner. She said: 'Dad, this is George, he's my best friend.' And I thought: 'God! What is he doing hanging around with fifteen-year-old girls?' I don't think she fancied him, she just liked him very much.

"The fact is that, even though I didn't much like some of her friends, I knew how Anna and her friends felt. Once you turn about fourteen you feel like you should be doing things. You're old enough to go out alone, to go out at night without your parents. The trouble is that, until you reach eighteen, there's nowhere to go, apart from the movies and the shops.

"I've just turned eighteen and I can legally go to pubs and clubs, I can go anywhere I like and dance and meet people and have fun. When you're younger there's nothing.

"There are youth groups but you have to have friends who are interested to belong to them.

"I can understand why raves are attractive to kids. They are a place to go and dance without worrying much about having to show a driver's licence or proof of age.

"As well as that, most of us are in the situation where all through our lives our fathers have been coming home from a hard day's work and saying: 'Give me a beer. Aah, that feels so much better.' So as your life becomes more stressed you decide you'll have a drink, because that's what you've learned to do. Then when you go out and you want to enjoy yourself, you know an alcoholic drink will make you feel better, the way it made the grown-ups in your life feel better. So you have one. It's a natural progression.

"Our social structure says you don't just have a good time. You have a stimulant of some kind when you want to enjoy yourself.

"In our family alcohol was never restricted, so to have a glass of wine or some beer with dinner was never a big deal. As a result, Anna and I rarely wanted it.

"The trouble with smoking is that it's not exciting enough for young people. It's just something you do, something that everyone tries at some stage. It's a natural progression to move on to something with more appeal, with more risk attached. So you try marijuana. The trouble with risking marijuana is that it can lead to other things.

"Our parents talked to us about drugs at the dinner table. Mum told us she had tried marijuana and we had a big discussion about why it was so popular in the sixties. She actually told us this after Anna and I had tried it and we didn't mention we had. The deed was done, why make a big deal of it?

"I thought Anna had huge self-esteem, she had everything. It wasn't her self-esteem that led her to experiment with drugs. It was fashion – and the fact that drugs are so easily available.

"Ultimately it was Anna's decision to put that pill in her mouth. If only she had known what I know now I am positive her decision would have been different.

"Her friends Alexia and Chloe were irresponsible in their behaviour. They had no time for schoolwork and, for reasons in their own lives, their self-esteem was pretty poor. All they were interested in was drugs and boys and talking about what they were doing.

"Anna was a virgin. We talked about it. We're sisters. She told me. She wasn't mature enough to be interested in sex or relationships and she had never been put in the situation where she had to make a decision about it.

"Anna already had some very special friends when Alexia sort of powered her way into Anna's life. Then Chloe came. Chloe idolised Anna. My sister was everything that Chloe wasn't – confident, beautiful, popular. Chloe had just changed schools and Anna was nice to her. Anna was always nice to people who needed friends – she gave them lots of chances.

"Anna really cared about people. That's why she had so many 'best friends' and they all meant the world to her. She was so caring and friendly that people were attracted to her. She always had time for the underdog and always made them feel happier about themselves.

"Anna used to tease me about being a real Goody Two Shoes. It was mainly because I did quite well at school and she wasn't an academic.

"I've always been fairly anti-drugs but I think in my generation I am in the minority. Over the last couple of years I have been hearing so much talk about drugs. In my economics class everyone was constantly discussing what raves so and so went to and what they took when they were there and how they felt the next day.

"'Honestly, I was having the best night,' one girl said to me. 'But what happened the next day?' I asked her. 'Oh, I vomited for a few hours,' she said. I thought, like: 'Oh *gross*!'

"The strong anti-drug feelings that I was getting tempted me in my last year of school. I talked about it to a close friend and we decided that our Higher School Certificate year was too important to throw away but that we might try ecstasy some time next year. Not once did it occur to me that if I ever actually took one of those tablets I could be doing myself serious harm. That's how ignorant we were, just a few weeks ago.

"Our ignorance is typical of the mentality of many young people in our society. Nobody really understands how dangerous and addictive drugs are. I had drug education at school. It consisted of watching some episodes of *Degrassi Junior High* in Year Nine and hearing a talk by two former heroin addicts at a Year Eleven camp. It didn't affect me much. They said they had been addicts and now they were married with families. We all thought: 'So what?'

"I realised over the last couple of years that a lot of people in my generation were trying drugs. I didn't agree with it then and I certainly don't now. People deny that drugs are addictive if they use them on a recreational basis but because they are mind-altering, they don't realise just how great the desire becomes and what damage they are doing to themselves.

"At first I was very angry with Anna for taking that ecstasy tablet. I thought she was too smart for that. But really, I can understand why she did it. First, it was so easily available. Second, her friends were taking it and enjoying themselves and raving about it. Nothing bad that she could see was happening to them. At fifteen especially, you don't think: 'Well, this could kill me so I won't take it.' At fifteen you think you are invincible.

"About six months before she died, Anna and her friends went to see a friend who was in hospital because she had taken drugs – speed or LSD, I'm not sure. The girl had a complete mental breakdown. They saw what drugs had done to her, but in the end even that didn't stop them.

"Fortunately for me, when I was fifteen I didn't have friends who used drugs and I already had doubts of my own. I had seen people I knew change over a short period of time when they started using drugs.

"Maybe it was because Anna had just left school that she decided to take ecstasy. Maybe she felt she had a job, that she was grown-up and that she was old enough to try something new. I'm not sure if it was the first or second time she had tried ecstasy. I know she'd been out with those people and they'd all tried it. She said *they* had a really good time but she never mentioned whether she had taken any. I never thought to ask. It didn't occur to me because I thought Anna was too smart.

"She was home a lot in the two weeks she had off after she left school. I was at home too, because I was studying for the HSC. She didn't have a lot to do and one day she was so bored she said: 'Alice, let's do some cooking.' So we got out potatoes and made chips. And she was so impatient, she could never wait for anything, so she just threw the slices into the oil and we both got splashed. We had matching burns.

"Whenever she made up her mind to do something, Anna couldn't wait. She was so flighty, she changed her mind every five minutes. But she was only fifteen and a young fifteen-year-old at that. If she hadn't decided to take ecstasy she would still be here today, probably poking her nose into the fridge or slamming her bedroom door.

"Anna wasn't an angel, but we didn't want an angel. We wanted her just the way she was. We always will."

4

JULIE'S STORY

The year Julie Leclerc spent in Australia changed her forever. Within twelve months she experienced overwhelming kindness and heartbreaking tragedy. She could be forgiven for regarding her stay as her worst nightmare come true, but instead, the eighteen-year-old French Canadian said her time here had made her a more responsible and mature person.

Dark-haired, unconsciously voluptuous and strikingly lovely, her face as exotic as her accent, Julie came to Sydney from Quebec as an exchange student at the beginning of 1995. When they discovered she was homesick and unhappy, Angela and Tony Wood invited her to move into their home to live with them and their daughters. Julie settled in beautifully, going to school with Anna and Alice and growing increasingly fond of her Australian "family".

Then, one Sunday morning she woke up to the news that Anna was in hospital, and that she wasn't expected to live.

Throughout the days of horror which followed and the weeks and months of mourning which continued until the end of her twelve-month stay in Sydney, Julie never left Angela, Alice and Tony Wood. She was with them beside Anna's hospital bed, she kept vigil in their broken home. She turned down offers of other places to stay, refusing to return to Quebec earlier than planned.

Julie had shared the good times with the Wood family. Now she shared the bad. She was their "daughter" and they loved her for it.

"I met Alice at school and we became friends. It was when I was visiting her home, with some other girls, that Angela, Alice's mother, noticed I was feeling sad. My host family was not working out. We were not happy with each other.

"Angela said I could come and live with them. They made a room for me which used to be for spare things. After the necessary paperwork was done, I moved in. They were very welcoming to me and I was much happier.

"The first time I met Anna was here, at a party. The next day I saw her at McDonald's in the morning before school. She waved to me and called to me to go and sit with her and her friends. She was really friendly.

"Everyone in the Wood family was nice to me when I came here to live. Anna showed me where the breakfast cereals were and how to find everything I needed. Within a week I felt like one of the family. In the beginning I was friendlier with Alice, who is the same age as me. Then we were doing our own things. I was meeting other exchange students from all over the world. There were no drugs or drinking under age at these gatherings. The exchange program is very strict about that. If you break the rules, you get sent home.

"My father is a policeman. I had tried drugs four times when I was younger, but with my family it was not a sensible thing to do. When I grew older I lost three friends in one year through drug-related suicide. That taught me all I needed to know about taking drugs.

"While I lived with the Woods I had a job as a waitress after school. I hated this job and it was good to get home. Tony would be there, cooking dinner. Alice was usually studying for her HSC. Anna and I began talking a lot. We became close. She never showed any jealousy at all about me being there.

"She tried to cheer me up about my horrible job. Tony did too. They were very funny. They had exactly the same sense of humour.

"Once we spent a whole day together at home, just the two of us. We talked the whole time. She tried to say to me there were spirits in the house. She tried to scare me. We had so much fun. I smoke and Anna came outside with me that day to have a cigarette. She didn't do it much. She was going to a local party with her friends that night and she became really worried that I was going to be alone when she left, as nobody else was home.

"She went to the party, still worrying, and after two hours she came home to check on me. 'Julie,' she said, 'I hope you are happy.'

"Anna tried drugs because she was only fifteen and at fifteen you want to do something new and different. She had the wrong friends.

"On Anna's last night at home she came downstairs wearing her blue jeans and a black jumper. She had no make-up – she was gorgeous, she didn't need any. She hugged everybody. I noticed how she hugged every one of us. She was so excited.

"I love this family very much. I would do anything for them. The whole family has been blown apart by this thing that happened to their daughter.

"I went with them to the hospital every day. Tony asked me to look after Alice when he couldn't be there for her. It was a terrible time for them. I offered to move out but Angela and Tony said no. They said: 'It would be even worse if you left us too.'"

Julie returned to Quebec in January 1996.

5

KATHIE'S STORY

Kathie* is a slender fifteen-year-old girl, with round brown eyes, clear skin and sleek straight chestnut hair which frames her small face like a cap. She lives in a household of women – her mother, who is divorced, her mother's friend and her sister. She sees her father regularly and gets on well with both her parents.

Kathie speaks in short no-nonsense sentences. She has been described by those who know her well as being strong-willed, and dominating. From outward appearances, Kathie seems like a sensible and well-adjusted girl, prefect material, the sort of person adults rely upon to set a good example. But Kathie also has a secret, deeply passionate self which adults don't know too much about, and this is almost certainly why she and Anna Wood were attracted to each other from the start.

"I was Anna's best friend.

"We've been together for four years, since the beginning of high school. We just clicked straight away. In the first two years of high school it was accepted that if Anna and Kathie were together – leave them alone. It was just the two of us. People knew that.

"We stayed just as close right through school, but over the next couple of years we began letting the others in. Alexia came first. We used to sit on the oval and she started to hang out there with us. She was very funny and open and our friendship was sort of spiritual. Then Chloe came from another school and we were a bit cruel to her at first. She was funny – sort of unco-ordinated and a bit goofy. We laughed at her. Then one day Anna decided to take her out, so we took her to Chatswood and from then she stayed with us.

"Then Sarine joined us. We had always known her but it wasn't until then that something pulled us all together. Sarine was very quiet. Anna always noticed when people needed attention. So we ended up with a group of five – Alexia, Chloe, Sarine, Anna and me. We spent time with kids from the rest of the year as well and we all had friends outside of school. But in school we kept our group to a minimum.

"We used to sit on the oval and just talk – about boys mainly and going out, and clothes and when we were younger. We'd talk about our parents, especially if we had a fight with them. Anna would be cranky because her mum made her stay and unpack the dishwasher or something like that. Or she wouldn't be allowed to go out. I'd say to her: 'Your mum's okay – she's just trying to take care of you.' The next day I'd be fed up with my mum and Anna would say the same thing to me.

"Anna and her mum got on really well most of the time. She used to talk to her a lot about everything.

"When I went over to Anna's house we would sit up for hours at night and she would tell me stories about England. We made plans for the future. She said she would love to go back there with me and we would open a shop. It would be a joint fashion and beauty shop – she was going to be a beautician so she would do the beauty and I would do the clothes.

"Anna wasn't very into relationships with boys – she wanted to be free and happy. She liked Toby, they were a couple for a while. They went out twice, I think. She said she loved the thrill of the chase, she loved knowing she could get a guy, but then when they gave in it was boring and she didn't want them any more.

"Most of the time we hung out at friends' houses and watched videos; we popped outside now and then for a cigarette. I've been smoking for years. In Year Seven Anna told me to stop, she said it wasn't good for me. So I stopped. Then I caught her having a cigarette. I was surprised. We did it because it was cool, but we didn't keep smoking all the time. Just now and then.

"We tried drink a bit later on. I've been drunk on Bacardi. You get it from people's older brothers and sisters, when there's a party. Sometimes the parents will be there but mostly people have get-togethers when their parents are away for the weekend.

"We also used to go go-kart racing a lot.

"I've only smoked marijuana twice. Even if you don't use drugs you know who has it, the people who provide it are very well known. I get an allowance. It's sort of been cut down at the moment but I used to get $200 a month, which was for my lunches every day at school and my clothes and going out at weekends. I would budget that out and go without something if I wanted to buy drink or cigarettes or drugs.

"I have tried ecstasy. I was at a friend's house and someone just had one of them. They're very expensive – sixty dollars.

"It made me feel very loving. I wanted to hug everything and touch everything. They call it the 'hug drug'. There was this tingling sensation. I smiled all the time and everything seemed beautiful and exaggerated. I didn't realise it was dangerous. They put drugs and the rave scene on such a high pedestal and like, no one tells you the bad points about it. I always ask when I try something, 'Has anyone ever got sick from taking this? What has happened to people? What can happen?' – because I have no knowledge of these things. Of course, because they're trying to sell it, they say: 'Oh no, nothing bad ever happens.' It's glorified.

"The people who say it's great are usually kids who have tried it or are dealing it or using it. They're usually a bit older.

"It's cool to have a drink or go out and get stoned. It's what you do if you want to be socially accepted. You also take it out of curiousity. People are telling you all the time that it's so good. If there are big signs up about the danger of drugs it's just another sign to me and to most people.

"We had another group outside of school, which is how we met George. There was Chloe, Alexia, Anna and me and George and his friend, Pete*. We became very close friends. We used to meet up at the shopping centre after school.

"Whenever we talked about drugs, Anna was very wary. Taking ecstasy would be wicked, she knew that. But she naturally wanted to know if what everybody said about it was true. The point is, she wouldn't have taken it if it wasn't available.

"I didn't go with them to the rave party. I didn't want to. In any case, I could never get around my mother to go to something like that.

"What happened to Anna has affected quite a few people. But there are others who have been doing it for so long and didn't know Anna very well and they won't believe ecstasy is dangerous. One of their close friends will have to die or have a really bad experience before they stop.

"This tragedy has made me see that I should love life more because you never know what's going to happen. I won't ever touch drugs again.

"I wish we could just blow up every single drug on this earth."

Kathie's mother, Anne, subscribes to the belief that today's parents indulge their children to compensate for the attention they are not providing.

"We are all more stressed, a lot of us are tight for money, many of us are divorced, and that makes us very vulnerable when it comes to disciplining our kids.

"At the same time we are living in an age of self-awareness; we know we are stuffed up so we are taking time out to work on ourselves.

"Meanwhile, we don't impose standards of behaviour on our kids, we don't discipline them, because we feel guilty that we are not spending enough time on them.

"They make demands on you, you give in despite your doubts – and you are lost.

"Kathie would have gone to that rave party if she could. But we are very close and as soon as she asked me if she could 'sleep over at a friend's house' that night, I knew she was hiding something. When I questioned her further, she couldn't tell me where 'the friend' even lived.

"Whenever she is asking me if she can do something that is a bit doubtful, she talks fast and is very vague. I always tell her to hang on, slow down, and start again. If she is lying she ends up laughing. She just can't do it.

"The more questions you ask your teenagers, the harder it is for them to lie. If you just say 'Yes' the minute they want you to agree to something, you make it easy for them to get away with lying.

"You have to keep talking to them.

"I always ask for the name and phone number of the girl whose house she is planning to visit and I often check with one of the other parents. Actually, I have been trying to stop these sleep-overs. They're not a good idea.

"Two weeks before Anna died, a similar situation had arisen over a plan the girls had to go go-kart racing with George. They were supposed to be going back to Alexia's to sleep. When I asked Kathie if Alexia's mother had agreed, she admitted that Maria* was going to be away that evening – there would be no parent in the house.

"I said she couldn't go and rang Angela Wood. We grounded the girls and they had the poohs with us for days.

"I didn't get around to checking with Angela on the night they were planning to go to the rave party. I wish I had.

"In the four years that I knew Anna I never heard her say a bad word about anybody. I never saw her in a foul mood. I can picture her always, with her backwards beret and her big smile. She'd bounce in, she and Kathie would go off to the shops, then they'd walk home and Anna would say: 'Hi, Mum' – she called me Mum – 'can you give us a smoke?'

"I would let them have a cigarette out on the deck. They were going to do it anyway and I preferred them to smoke here rather than in public. A young girl walking down the street with a cigarette in her hand conveys a certain image. I'm aware that this is a very sexist view, but it's one we won't change in my lifetime.

"Anna was a lovely lovely kid and instead of mourning her death we should be celebrating the happiness of her life."

6

EDDIE, TOBY, GAYLE AND IAN

Friendly, cheerful and interested in everyone, Anna Wood burst into her first year of high school like sunshine and shared her warmth with a host of brand new friends. Few of the girls she had met in her last few months of primary school in Belrose came to The Forest High and she had spent most of the previous four years living in England. But true to form, Anna's fellow Year Seven students were attracted to her like clichéd bees to a warm jar of golden honey.

The lid was never on. Anna had something for everyone.

Dropping Anna at school some mornings, her mother was fascinated at the way the girls all kissed and hugged each other when they met each day. It was different from the way friends had behaved during Angela's own youth in England and even during her earlier years in Australia.

Other parents, too, have remarked how teenagers, particularly girls, have become more unconsciously physical in their expression of affection for each other over the past ten years. One writer suggested that nineties children hug each other so much because their parents no longer hug them enough.

Among Anna's new friends was Eddie, a tall girl with a wide welcoming smile and a mane of golden blonde wavy hair. Eddie is now sixteen.

"I was Anna's best friend.

"It was about halfway through Year Seven when it happened. She and Kathie were close in a way, but Anna was the sort of person I had always wanted to have for a friend and I was so happy that she wanted me as a friend as well.

"We talked about everything. I could tell Anna my deepest, darkest secrets and it would never get out. She could be trusted. If Anna told me not to do something, I wouldn't do it.

"She was unusual, not the same as other girls. I argued with my parents, we all did, but she *loved* her parents. They were more understanding than most parents. If you had a problem, her whole family sat down and listened to you. They were such friendly people.

"She had holidays with me and my family; she came to stay with us at the beach, and I went camping with her family. We practically lived at each other's houses. We never ran out of things to talk about.

"Anna was never influenced by others. There's no way you could say she was easily led. Nobody could change her mind about anything and if she didn't want to do something, she wouldn't.

"Other people came into our group and back in those early days of high school I suppose you would describe us as a bad crowd. The whole of our year was very close. We would kiss on the cheek when we arrived at school, and hug and everything. We were always very happy but we were very hyper all the time and maybe we were a bit disruptive.

"Anna was popular with the boys as well as the girls. All the guys had a crush on her but they never got her. She was interested in a few of them but not interested enough – it always fizzled out.

"She didn't have a lot of money to spend – she didn't get pocket money and she didn't have a job. Her parents just gave her the money she needed if we wanted to go out.

"Anna and I thought we were really good when we started smoking. Even then, she said to me: 'Eddie, never go anywhere past this.'

"We did though. I tried a little marijuana when I was twelve or thirteen. I had heard it wasn't as bad for you as smoking. In school, in Personal Development and Health, they told us not to smoke or drink, but you never hear about the bad things that can happen to you if you take drugs.

"PD/Health was our bludge period anyway.

"It's not enough for them just to say *Don't*. If there was a really good book about kids and drugs I'd read it. We need to be given things that make us think about the drug issue.

"If I had wanted to try drugs I would have had no trouble getting them. It would have been so easy. Some of the other kids at school have them. The teachers have no idea they are around. You can also get them at the shopping centre.

"After two years at Forest I left; my parents sent me to a Christian school. I still saw Anna at the shops; we kept in touch but it wasn't as easy.

"When I left Anna gave me a card that said: 'If you ever forget me, you're busted.'

I'm never going to forget her."

Toby no longer goes to school. He left high school halfway through Year Nine, then completed Year Ten at a TAFE college. He now works full-time at a restaurant and lives with his parents. He spends a lot of time with some older friends with whom he works. He is a pale, neatly dressed youth with light-coloured under-cut hair. At sixteen, he sounds older than his years.

"Anna and I were close friends for a long time. I met her when I started at Forest High in Year Eight. She had this wonderful smile, she was such a bouncy girl, and always happy. We started going out – what the older generation calls 'going steady'. She was my girlfriend. She was twelve at the time and I would have been thirteen.

"We used to talk a lot. I would go to her home and talk for hours. I used to talk to her mum, Angela, as well.

"We broke up after a while but we stayed friends. Then we got together again in Year Nine. We spent hours on the phone.

"Anna was a very down-to-earth girl. She knew what she was talking about. If she didn't like something somebody was doing she would tell them – but she'd do it with a smile on her face.

"She was a very physical girl, always kissing and cuddling you. She'd come up to you with that big smile and say: 'Hi Cutie,' and give you a big kiss. But she was very young in her ways. She was like a child compared with a lot of the girls her age.

"When I left school we still called each other all the time. We would talk about how she was going, what I was doing. She would often ring me when she was baby-sitting. Sometimes she was allowed to come out with me and my friends and we would drive around.

"During that last year I was going out with somebody else but Anna and I remained close. When I broke up with my girlfriend, Anna came with my friends and me for a couple of drives around the beaches.

"I started smoking in Year Eight and haven't stopped since then. I rarely drink alcohol. My parents and I belong to the Baha'i religion so our house is an alcohol-free zone.

"I have tried marijuana. I had half an ecstasy pill once and I didn't like it – I didn't like the 'downs'. I always knew something could stuff up as well. Anything can happen if you take those things. Look at ecstasy. They said it was a nice clean-cut drug. Obviously they were wrong.

"The people who are pushing drugs are older people. They make batches of them and sell them to younger kids who sell them to their friends. So you have a couple of very rich kids and a whole lot of other kids running around all spun-out.

"Kids know drugs are dangerous but when their parents tell them not to do them, it makes them want to do it more.

"I haven't touched any illegal drugs for a year now. The friends I hang out with don't do drugs or anything. I work with these two older guys, one's eighteen and one's twenty. They have both tried it and they have both warned me off. They told me how bad it can be. Taking drugs is like hanging off a cliff and wondering what will happen if you let go. There's the feeling of freedom – but no-one can say for sure what will happen when you land.

"On the day Anna died I was having a fine day until my ex-girlfriend rang me and told me what had happened.

"I just couldn't believe it. I started walking, I walked and walked and tried to work it out. Anna was the last person I expected to have done that. I always had this feeling that some day someone was going to go because of drugs – but not Anna. She was always so anti-drug, so against it. On the other hand, she must have taken ecstasy of her own free will. You can't force someone to take a drug. I guess she must have suddenly thought: 'Oh, what the hell?' That would be like Anna.

"I walked right into a bush.

"I know that when I get old I will lose some of my friends. That they might die.

"This is too soon."

Gayle Parnaby hasn't been able to replace Anna at the beauty salon where she began what was to be the job of her dreams.

"We haven't been able to find another girl who looks so good, works so well and cares so much about people," said

55

Gayle, the owner and manager of the *Skinvogue* salon, at Belrose. "We haven't been able to find anyone with such sparkle.

"From the first day we met, Anna was perfect. She took the trouble to dress up and she looked fabulous for her interview. She shook my hand and said: 'I'm so pleased to meet you.' She did the same when she met my husband. Such good manners are not something you expect in a fifteen-year-old these days.

"She greeted our clients warmly and was never shy on the phone. She looked for work, always asking what else she could do. Nothing was a bother to her. She kept her eye on what I was doing and she brought me a coffee when I managed a break – and she always made sure it was hot! Not even my senior girls have ever done that!

"A friend of mine always tries out my new girls by ringing them up and asking for an embarrassing treatment. When he did it to Anna she said, very politely: 'Would you mind holding the line a moment please?' She put him on hold, opened her eyes wide and goggled at us all.

"'There's a man on the line,' she gasped, 'who says he wants his *bum* waxed!'

"The girls warned her that it was probably a prank call, so she went back to the phone and said as cool as you like: 'Hi. I'll just let you speak to Gayle.'

"My friend was roaring with laughter. 'She's perfect,' he said. 'Keep her.' She was, too.

"She was so thrilled when I let her have a go at tinting my eyelashes that Saturday and she did it so well. I have so much trouble believing that bubbly little girl who ran out of here that afternoon went in to a dance in the city and took drugs. She just wasn't the type!

"The day after Anna died her mother came to see us here. She said to me: 'Go home and hold your children. Love them every

56

minute, as much as you can, because you never know how long you'll have them.' On such a terrible day, Angela was thinking about the rest of us, and how we were feeling. She has incredible warmth and strength. Anna would have been just the same."

Anna Wood's ability to make a special friend of everyone she met bridged the generations. Ian Ralston, a relatively new friend of the Wood family, with two adult children of his own, sent them the following letter a few weeks after Anna's death.

"I mainly remember Anna because I can't forget her. Because of her untimely death, she is regularly on my mind. But I used to sometimes think about her before then.

"Anna was less than a third of my age, a kid, but she was easy to talk to – she could start a conversation. She didn't try to be older than her years but she made me feel a lot younger than mine!

"I will never forget the way Anna would greet you with a hug and a peck on the cheek, as if you were a relative. More than anything I will not forget chatting to her on several occasions. We had a good chin-wag on New Year's Eve, 1994. I don't remember the details of our conversation, I just remember sitting next to her on the lounge, eating some good food and enjoying a good chat. It seemed to me that the generation gap had closed.

"I didn't know Anna all that well, but well enough to know I liked her a lot. I am very saddened that I, in fact none of us, will ever have the opportunity to know her better. She made an indelible impression on me as a young girl so full of life.

"God bless you, Anna Wood."

7

CHLOE'S STORY

Chloe lives in a large two-storey house in the next street to the Wood family. It's a light and modern home, attractively furnished, with gleaming tiles, pale rugs and pretty furniture. It was here that Chloe brought her friend, Anna, when she became ill after taking ecstasy.

It's a shock to discover Chloe looking fragile and painfully vulnerable. She has a small face and porcelain, almost translucent skin. Her large black jumper swamps her frame. She has a mop of reddened hair and clear, sky-blue eyes. She looks more like a victim than a villain, a bit player for whom the leading role in this tragedy has been too much of a burden.

A brand new kitten clings to her neck. It's a gift from her parents, to cheer her up. She turned sixteen in December 1995.

Her mother runs a shop during the day; her father works at night.

Chloe is quiet and apparently frank, although her power of recall is not what it was. She looks tired. Now and then, when a pleasant memory stirs, a low chuckle creeps into her throat and she looks surprised to find it there.

"I was Anna's best friend.

"We were all special to her, but Anna and I were closest. It's hard to explain.

"I used to go to a Catholic girls' school but I didn't like it. I changed from group to group and I didn't make any close friends there. I wanted to go to Forest High and I talked my parents into it.

"I didn't even know about drugs when I was at the convent and I was, like, totally against smoking. I never thought about doing the wrong thing.

"When I first came to my new school at the start of Year Nine, I had a big fight with Anna and her group. I met some other people, out of school, and I tried smoking and drinking for the first time. People say to you: 'D'you want to have a cigarette?' and you just say: 'Okay.' Then it's 'Okay' to a drink and to the other stuff they offer you. They always tell you how great it is and you don't really question them. They use it and they're okay.

"Then Anna made friends with me. We were all very close after that and we didn't let any others in. People would comment on how close we were, the five of us – Kathie, Alexia, Sarine, Anna and me. Of course, Anna had heaps of other close friends too. Everyone liked her. But they weren't in our group.

"I don't really know why I got into drugs. I haven't got all those reasons people usually talk about. My home life is perfect. I live with my mum and dad and my older brother and sister. My grandmother lives here too, in her flat. I've been given every-thing I ever wanted – I learned saxophone, piano, guitar. I had dancing lessons, I played netball and tennis. I was a straight-A student at my old school. I did especially well in science, logic and philosophy.

"I had some drug education in Year Seven and Year Eight at my old school but I didn't think about it when I started taking stuff. The drug education at Forest was hopeless. There was one lesson in Personal Development and Health – I think we were in

Year Nine – where they listed the drugs and said they were bad for you. We just mucked around while it was going on.

"We were told: 'This is marijuana, these are cigarettes, these are amphetamines, don't do it.' They never gave you details. They didn't tell you the bad things, or give you the street names of the drugs. It didn't mean anything to me. I never thought about it. I mean, I suppose drugs are illegal for some reason or other, but at the time, that's not the way you think.

"Anna thought about it. It's just that none of us were very smart and Anna was different. She was smart. She had a life. She had a future.

"I never thought what I was doing was dangerous or wrong. I was in a huge hurry to grow up.

"Anna and Kathie were the first ones in the group to start smoking. I had started smoking too, and drinking, by the time I joined them. The first time I tried dope I was at Anna's house. Her parents were out for the day and everyone was out the back – we all tried it. I didn't like marijuana much; it made me feel sick.

"In the past year I've tried cigarettes, drink, dope, speed, ecstasy and tripping. Tripping is when you use LSD. You hallucinate. You can see things more deeply. Reality isn't reality any more. The problem with tripping is that you can get stuck on a trip so that you can never get back to normal. None of us liked tripping that much.

"E [ecstasy] makes you feel good. The music you are listening to sounds better, everything you touch feels good. You love the world. You want to hug complete strangers. You need a cuddly toy or something to hug. I've also used speed. It's white powdery stuff that gives you energy.

"I never got sick off those kind of drugs. I never vomited. I just felt pretty scattered. It's just like your brain has died for a while afterwards. You're just like: 'What? D'uh?' all day.

"It was easy to get what I needed. Not at school – actually most of the kids at school who did drugs only tripped or choofed. That's LSD or marijuana. The dealers, the ones selling speed and Es, aren't usually at school but they are around the area or at the shopping centre. They're boggos – they're all hopeless. I mean, they're not, like, bitchy or mean or harmful to you or anything like that. They just have no hope in their lives. They're drug-stuffed.

"It's easy to just go over to them or phone them at home and you speak in a sort of code and you get them to line you up with something. Once they know you choof or whatever, they know you won't dob them in.

"I hated all the wheeling and dealing. I wished it wasn't necessary. I just wanted the feeling, the way it felt when you were on something, but not all the trouble and worry.

"My life changed when I got into drugs. I wagged school and I ran away from home a couple of times. I just stopped caring; my life just went downhill. The first boy I slept with was a friend but after that I slept with three or four others, quite a lot of boys I think, over a period of three or four months. It was always when I was under the influence of drugs. I was happy being miserable. I didn't want help.

"Anna was worried about me taking drugs so much. She never wanted us to do it.

"We all know ourselves why we take drugs but none of us can really say why Anna finally decided to take ecstasy that night.

"Anna didn't do drugs like we did. She smoked some pot over the last nine months or so but apart from that she might have had one trip, at a fireworks night – she didn't like it – and I think she tried speed once. She took half an ecstasy tablet about a month before she passed away. We were at a local rave party. Her parents didn't know and it wasn't far from home so she would have just said she was staying with one of us for the night.

"Anna met George through my brother. George is older than us – about nineteen. We started hanging out with him and his mate, Pete, at the shopping centre – Anna and me, Alexia, Kathie, George and Pete. We called ourselves the Baboonas. We were like a club.

"When we were together, Anna acted like our mother. She had morals and her own way of thinking and she wouldn't change it. If you didn't think the way she did, you weren't worth it. Her attitude was always: 'This is what I think and if you don't agree you can just leave.' Anna had her own way of working things out, and in the end she was always pretty much right.

"We could never lie to Anna. She was the heart of our group and we all loved her.

"She was worried about me dropping out of school and running away from home and worrying my parents. She knew how much I wanted to be an actress. I love drama and theatre. I had always planned to go to the National Institute of Dramatic Art when I left school. Two weeks before she passed away, Anna said to me: 'What would really make me happy is if you went back to school and did your HSC and then went to NIDA and won your first acting award for me.'

"So that's what I've decided to do. The teachers say I've got the brains, it's just that I haven't been trying.

"At first, after Anna passed away, I didn't give a shit about life any more. I stopped taking drugs because I was scared after what happened to her but I drank to excess and I slept with people while I was drunk and I lost all my morals.

"The only people I still care about are my mum and dad. They were so great when it was all happening, they had kids in and out of the house for weeks and they trusted us and they supported us.

"I ended up telling my mother everything I had been doing – the drugs, the drinking, and that I'd had sex and everything. She's been helping me to get my life back under control. I'm seeing a psychiatrist and we're trying to work out why I've been like this. But also, I'm sort of finding a purpose in my life.

"I'm going to be an actress but I'd also like to do something about drug education. I wouldn't mind gathering a lot of kids my age around me and telling them that drugs suck.

"If I had been told E could kill you I certainly would not have touched it. If someone from my own age group had warned me I would have listened.

"You know, there are a lot of kids around who don't do drugs. I used to think everyone did but there are quite a lot who don't. Or who did and have stopped because they found out how bad it can be.

"When new Year Sevens start high school I'm going to tell them about drugs. Me and a guy who hasn't done drugs, we're going to talk to them together.

"I've given up all the illegal stuff now. I'm all greened out. The only things I'm still having are cigarettes and vodka if I need a bit of a lift. I'm taking anti-depressants.

"I've stopped lying to my parents and I've had some really good nights without anything at all.

"I went back to school for our Year Ten formal at the end of the year. Anna had been on the organising committee. She had drawn up this contract for everyone to sign, stating we would not have drugs at the formal, that it would be straight. So we all signed it and we all went straight.

"We had a fabulous time. Anna would have been proud of us."

Chloe's mother discovered that her daughter had been taking drugs a month before Anna Wood died.

"I felt so stupid. All the signs were there but I just didn't realise.

"My sister had told me Chloe's behaviour was erratic. She had run away from home twice. She never came home from school until tea-time. She was a top student in Year Seven, a brilliant debater and actress. She played netball and did physical culture. Then she changed schools and she didn't open a book for two years.

"I still didn't suspect she was lying to me. Not until the night when she rang and told me she had taken an ecstasy tablet and that she was ill and needed to be picked up.

"I always thought we were best friends. I thought we were close. Perhaps I spoilt her. I'm a very trusting person and Chloe has a very strong personality.

"She has never screamed at me or sworn in the house. She doesn't behave resentfully in any way. She just goes off. She leaves home.

"I am away at work all day, but my husband is here. My mother is here. I have raised my twenty-one-year-old daughter and my nineteen-year-old son the same way I raised Chloe and they have given me no trouble.

"Chloe ran away for the first time at the end of Year Nine. My husband and I had gone away by ourselves for the first time in twenty-five years to celebrate our silver wedding anniversary. Her sister drove her to the shops and Chloe didn't come home. She ran away again after the school had rung me to report that she'd been wagging lessons. When I asked her about it, she walked out. She slept on the streets or in some old school building for two nights, until we found her.

"On the night Anna died I didn't know where Chloe was going and I didn't ask. I had decided it was better for her to go off on her own, knowing she would still want to come home to us, than to drive her away again by questioning her whereabouts.

"When I first found out Chloe was taking drugs I sent her to a drug and alcohol counsellor. She didn't like her. Since Anna died Chloe has been seeing a psychiatrist.

"Anna Wood was a really sweet kid, very bubbly and happy. She called me Mum.

"I thought how easily it could have been Chloe."

Three weeks after this conversation, Chloe discovered she was pregnant.

"It must have happened after Anna passed away, when I didn't know what I was doing for a lot of the time – although I do know my boyfriend and I were doing it safely, so I don't know what went wrong.

"I've broken up with him now anyway. He says it was all my fault and all that and he shouldn't have to be responsible.

"I know what Anna would have done. She would have given me a lecture and then we would both have cried and then she would have told me to make the best of it. I don't think she would have let me have an abortion.

"I couldn't give my baby up for adoption. I've already lost Anna. I couldn't bear to lose something else that really is a part of me.

"My parents have been wonderful. They are the best parents I've met. Mum was going to give up her business anyway, to spend more time with me. Now she is going to help me look after my baby so I can go back to school and study for my Higher School Certificate.

"We're both really happy and excited. I've given up drinking and I'm not taking anti-depressants any more. I have to look after myself and the baby.

"I've changed my plans to be an actress. Did you know only one per cent of actors in this country are regularly employed? I have to have a stable job if I'm going to be supporting a child.

"I might go to university and study law. Then some day I might get to be in the government. There's a lot of things about this life that I would like to change."

8

ALEXIA'S STORY

She orders her mother to bring her an ashtray, and arranges it
beside a wine glass which turns out to contain diet cola. It's all
Alexia ever drinks these days, unless she's out, in which case she
might just have a couple of Midoris. She's been reading, she
says, just dipping into this paperback she picked up at the
second-hand book shop, looking for a little wisdom. It's called
The Psychology of Consciousness. The pages are yellowing and
smell of mould.

Since her parents' volatile separation early in 1995, Alexia
has been living mainly with her mother and her nine-year-old
sister in a house tucked discreetly away from the road.

She hasn't been well so she is wearing a robe, but her lush
young body is better designed for the wide skirt and shoulder-
showing blouse of a Greek taverna. She has wide dark eyes, an
open smiling face, and she laughs breathlessly and often with
an infectious exuberance. She talks constantly, her words
rushing in on each other, the ends of her sentences washed
away in each new wave of enthusiastic thought which crashes
into her mind.

If Anna preferred to replace one word with twelve, Alexia
works with twenty or thirty or more. The police already have
several versions of her evidence in their reports. The only time
she is silent is when she concentrates, for a second or two, on the
tedious business of linking her words with fact.

Despite her womanly appearance and pseudo-adult tastes, for Alexia adolescence has not been easy. At fifteen she is the youngest in what was once Anna Wood's dynamic circle of friends. She is a child in crisis whose response to the death of the friend she undoubtedly loved with a passion has been to play out her own role in the drama with every ounce of energy she has.

"I was Anna's best friend.

"She called me her soul mate. We were inseparable, especially over the last two years. Actually we became friends a long time ago, years ago, when I was younger and first came to the school and I was having so much trouble adjusting to high school life and I was going from friend to friend. I'd always known Anna, we'd always talked, but one day I was crying and upset and she said: 'Hey Alex! Would you like to come and sit on the oval with us?' and I was like *wow*! I said: 'I'd *love* to!' And so I went down and after that she was always inviting me to join them, she always welcomed me. I was so shy but she brought me out of my shell with all those people, all her group.

"The five of us, me, Kathie, Sarine, Chloe and Anna, we weren't even like best friends, we were like sisters. We were closer than close, anybody who knew us would tell you. Everywhere we went at school, we all had to walk together, joined by the arms, together always. We couldn't even walk across the oval without holding on to each other, we were so so close.

"We had our fights but that's what kept us together. They say the ones that love you the most hurt you the most. Anna would say to me: 'Alex, you're not talking to me, I don't know what you're thinking, tell me what's wrong.' All our fights were when we were losing communication. We would always end up crying in each other's arms.

"One day we were in Hyde Park and me and Anna went for a walk and we just kept saying how much we loved each other and promising to never let our friendship end, to never let each other go. We had a special bond. When Anna felt pain, I felt it twice as bad. When she cried, all I'd want to do was cry too because I could feel her pain. The only time she felt pain was when her mum and dad would fight or something, but that didn't happen often. She'd get upset when she didn't do as well as she expected at school, because she had high hopes for herself.

"Oh but she'd have her moods all right, moods when she wouldn't want to talk, but that wasn't often either, she was Miss Hyperactive! She understood my bad days just as much as I understood her moods. I am not the sort of person who gets moody, I am the sort of person who gets depressed and I just close up and don't want to talk but Anna would make me talk and make me feel better and five minutes later I would be jumping up and down saying: 'You're so cute, thank you, thank you,' and I'd give her a big hug.

"It was, like, a real relationship. If we were sleeping over I would lie on the top bunk and she would be in the bottom and I'd call out: 'Goodnight, Gorgeous, I love you' and she'd say: 'Love you, too.' I could look like a beast, with pox on my face and my hair everywhere and she would walk in and not give a damn.

"I don't have much confidence about the way I look. I'd be thinking I was fat, I'd be thinking I was ugly, but Anna would say: 'Alex, put your hair up like this, hold your head like that, smile at me!' and she'd tell me I had beautiful hair and a beautiful smile and she would build me up and help me think better of myself. 'Hi, Gorgeous!' she'd say. I could wear what I want, feel how I want, tell her anything, I could trust her with anything. We always said that to each other. 'You're the only one

I really trust.' Anna and I had a tighter bonding than anyone else in the world.

"When my parents split up I was pretty upset. Anna was very supportive. She was supportive about every problem I had. She'd say: 'Come and stay at my house.' I loved her family life. It was such a wholesome household. They had great breakfasts, great dinners, they were always happy. It was so much better than here.

"We were doing seances and things in our spare time. We were interested in the unknown. The first thing we did whenever we woke up together was to ask each other about our dreams.

"One day Anna was here and she started telling me a big deep secret about her family and I said: 'Oh, I know, you told me three weeks ago' and I told her all that I already knew about it. She was standing in front of that window there, staring at me and she said: 'Alex! How do you know this? It only happened *yesterday*!' And I'm sitting here saying: 'Oh no! Oh no! Oh no!' And she's saying: 'Alex, Alex, you're scaring me, you're scaring me!'

"Doing drugs was the same sort of thing – exploring and expanding your mind. I wanted to reach new depths, that's how I got into them.

"Chloe was influenced by drugs first and when we saw her doing that we all got interested. We were so bewildered by what we saw. Chloe was having this wild time. It was a journey into the unknown, it was something to expand your mind, it made us think things we had never thought before. This is what we were all interested in doing – it was like the seances. We wanted to grasp hold of what other people didn't know and journey into it.

"Drugs were exciting to us. We knew a lot of people who did it and watching them made us think: 'Let's try it, let's try it.' We were all worried about it but everyone who used them told us it was a wonderful thing and they all seemed to be all right, you know? They told us about what they could feel and do on it and the places they saw and the people they met and it was all amazing to us.

"Of all of us Anna was the most wary. She didn't want to do it, she was worried, she said: 'Oh, guys, I don't know, I don't know.'

"We smoked pot a few times. We did it at each other's houses, outside obviously, so you couldn't smell it. We didn't do it much, just when our parents were at work and we were home in the school holidays, or when they went out at weekends. Sometimes we sat on the school oval because you could see if anyone was coming.

"Everyone else did dope all the time, like a daily thing. Lots of the kids at school smoked marijuana. You'd say: 'Where are you going?' and they'd say: 'Oh just out for a brew.' We didn't smoke it much, by comparison.

"We didn't usually have to buy pot. We just got it from some other kid at school. They'd just have it, along with their books and things. We didn't usually have to pay. If they were friendly they'd give you some. We never had any money. Only Kathie always had money.

"It was only dangerous because it was illegal. We never ever thought about it being dangerous to our bodies.

"In Year Seven we smoked to be cool. Then we tried marijuana, but we didn't like it much. By the time we were in Year Nine we couldn't stop smoking cigarettes. We were hooked. We would all put in a dollar fifty each and share a packet. Or we'd smoke Kathie's.

"Alcohol was never a big thing with any of us. If I go out, I drink socially – I would just ask for a couple of Midoris or something because that's a drink I enjoy. But we never did binge drinking."

"About Easter last year we met George at the shopping centre. I just started chatting to him, I'm a very friendly person, and I found out we were both Greek. I yelled out 'Oh! Baboonas!' and we became the Baboona clan, that's what we called ourselves.

"I don't actually think it means best buddies or anything like that. I think it means gorillas, as a matter of fact.

"It wasn't that George was a big older man sort of thing. We liked him because he was shy, he was pure, he had nothing to hide. Gentle! My God, that is the word! Gentle. So sweet! Do you know what? He wouldn't hurt a fly.

"He didn't get on with older people because he wasn't loud, he wasn't a wild party animal, he accepted us for who we were.

"None of us had a crush on him. He was our best friend. Look how bad I look at the moment. George wouldn't care. We had faith in George, he would never let us down, he never ever did.

"It was just fun. We all got on like a house on fire, we'd have no arguments, we'd all sit there and laugh our heads off at absolutely nothing.

"As far as sex goes, Anna was saving herself for a special person to come along. Most of us were. Virgins. Kind of. Just very recently I met a really nice guy and we were together for a very long time so I *was* having a very nice relationship with him. Anna said it was okay for us to go ahead because we were so in love.

"It upset Anna sometimes, me having a boyfriend. She'd say: 'Alex, Alex, come and spend some time with *me*!' And we'd end up crying. There was a slight problem but we worked it out in the end. She liked my boyfriend. He was older, the same age as George, but we've broken up now.

"It was the same year, when we were in Year Ten, that Chloe told us about ecstasy. We were curious. It was wild. People seemed to have such a good time on it.

"I wasn't satisfied with my life and with what I had. My life is so inadequate. I have been having huge problems at home. Even the police have had to come here. I don't have what everyone else has. I still don't but that's something I've got to live with.

"There was the problem with my parents, but other things as well, you know. Reality is a pressure for me and I wanted to release myself and I thought I could do it with ecstasy. So one night, me, Anna and Chloe went to a rave party with George and we decided to try ecstasy.

"We bought two tablets off this guy. We cut them in half and had half each.

"It worked for us all that night. We enjoyed it immensely. We were screaming and laughing and jumping around. The worst part was the next morning. We all felt pretty terrible then, of course, and we had nowhere to go because we were supposed to be sleeping over somewhere and it was too early to go home. I remember we went to a local park and just all sat there, trying to stay awake until about nine o'clock in the morning, feeling seedy and tired. We caught a bus home.

"Our parents thought we were at somebody's house.

"I was told ecstasy was the safest drug. I had already stopped taking acid – LSD – because you can get stuck on a trip for the rest of your life and the last time I took it, well I just took it one time to try it, but I was so scared that I spent the whole time thinking: 'I'm not getting off this, I'm not getting off it.' I was paranoid.

"The next time we took ecstasy was the night Anna got sick. It was about four months later.

"Anna was the one who told us to slow down with the drugs. Whenever we talked about whether we were going to try something, she'd say: 'Oh come on, let's not.'

"But that one night she wanted to do it, she was excited that she had been allowed to . . . I mean that she had been able to get out to go to a rave party. The idea of going to a frantic wild night was something she wanted to do.

"I'm not happy with the girl we got the ecstasy from, but I don't blame her for Anna's death. I know lots of people who are dealing drugs and – well, I don't know them *any more* but I did, when I was sometimes trying drugs. We could have got it from anyone. She was just one of so many people out there who are dealing.

"I blame myself too. I wish I had stronger willpower so I could have decided not to do drugs that night. I wish to God we had got help more quickly. But the thought that Anna might be dying never entered our heads that morning.

"I had a bit of drug education at school but it was at a time when I was having my problems and Personal Development and Health was such a boring class. I would sit up the back and not listen. Nobody listened – we all mucked around.

"What they should do is tell you how important PD/Health is; they should say it's a class that can save your life. I only remember them having a thing about drugs once and they didn't mention MDMA, which is ecstasy.

"If somebody had told me it could kill me, it could swell my brain the way it did to Anna, I'd be scared. If a teenager who had tried it told me about it, I'd have taken a lot more notice.

"We have a lot to say about the drug problem, we have been through it ourselves. The younger generation is more likely to listen to the younger generation. Kids don't listen to adults because most of us feel adults are just out to get us.

"Parents just say: 'You can't do it.' Full stop. Okay, so they may have their reasons, but we're not going to listen, are we?

"We're only kids.

"Anyway, our group is giving up drugs. On me Anna's death has had a big impact and I also know George, Kathie and Chloe won't ever touch drugs again.

"For our Year Ten farewell I wanted to write a big speech about Anna but they said it would make it too depressing. Her sister came in place of her. In the end I just said: 'Thanks to Anna Wood for being in our lives and for helping to make this formal such a great success.' You should have heard how everyone clapped and screamed.

"After that, Chloe and I went into the toilets and we had a bit of a cry and then we put our make-up on and went back again and just said: 'Sorry Anna, we just had to do that, you know we did.' Even at the formal I couldn't escape that feeling of emptiness I've had since she's been gone. Half of my body was devoted to her.

"I loved Anna. I understand her family's pain but I don't think they understand mine.

"If anyone ever needs someone to talk to about drug-taking, because they want to stop or because they think they are getting into it too much, I'll always be there for them. I'll try to advise them. I'll be there to help them.

"The trouble is that drugs is a world on its own. Once you're in there, it's very very hard to get out.

"And *that's* the truth."

On the night of the tragic rave party, Alexia's mother arrived home to find a note saying that her daughter and Anna were staying at George's house.

"I thought Alexia was staying at Anna's house that night. She had asked me if she could and I said yes, if it was okay with her mum.

"I knew the rave party was on. I already told Alexia she couldn't go. It's so hard saying no to these kids, you know? They don't listen. People don't understand . . . kids don't do what you tell them any more.

"It's incredible how many of these young kids are taking drugs. They smoke – it's cool. They take drugs – it's cooler. But not Anna. She was a lovely girl, like a daughter to me. She bought me flowers on my birthday. We were very close.

"She called me Mum."

9

GEORGE'S STORY

If this were fiction, he would be suave and wickedly handsome, arrogant and sensual, an ink-eyed seducer of young girls and vulnerable women.

In reality, as Angela Wood suggested, George is a gentle little guy. Alexia too was probably quite right when she said even flies could feel safe in his company. Unfortunately for both Anna Wood and George, the last time she was in his company she wasn't safe at all.

He is slightly built and sallow; he has crisp, neatly cut curls. He speaks quietly, uncertainly, and despite his smart, carefully conservative clothes, he has an apologetic manner. When asked to express an opinion on the drugs issue, George is open to suggestion about what those opinions ought to be. He's not a boy who likes to disagree.

George is nineteen, an apprentice tradesman who lives at home with his family.

His mother and father had no idea he took drugs. He was always a quiet, well-behaved boy, they said. He was never in trouble, he spoke to them with respect.

They didn't like him going to the dance parties, but to have a good time, a boy needed some excitement.

These days, they said, George comes home a lot earlier in the evening.

"I don't know why I was attracted to those girls or why they liked me. I just had so much fun being with all of them, sort of thing. I am the eldest in my family, older than all my cousins and everything, so all through my childhood I have been used to hanging around with people younger than me. Maybe that had something to do with it.

"I met them at a shopping centre in French's Forest. We didn't do anything much, we just talked and we all had fun, sort of thing. It wasn't until about August that we started going places together. We'd all jump in the car and just drive somewhere. I have a Mini. I liked taking them out in it.

"Even though I only knew them for a short period of time I felt as if I'd known them for years. I felt comfortable with them. They were so easygoing.

"In the last few weeks before she died, Anna and I became really close. She would call when I was at work and leave a message, like: 'Hi, how are you?' When I'd go to the shopping centre after knocking off work, usually to get some food, Anna was always there. We'd talk. If I had any problems or whatever, I'd talk to her about them. We became really close friends. She didn't have any problems to talk about.

"She had a big smile and big blue eyes. She would sit on my lap and say 'I want a cigarette' in Greek in a little baby voice. We taught her how to say that, Alexia and me.

"When people ask me why I started taking drugs, I have no answer. There was nothing wrong at home. It's the same thing as it is for people who drink to have a good time. I took drugs to have a good time.

"At first, ecstasy made me feel really happy and talkative. I'm sort of shy, I suppose. There is no real reason why I started taking it. I just felt like it. My family were shocked when I told them what I had been doing. I told them after Anna died.

"I was already getting bored with it by then, anyway. I've been to about thirty rave parties in the past year and for more than half of them I've been straight, sort of thing. I suppose I've taken ten or fifteen ecstasy tablets over that time.

"I'm off drugs now. That was my second-last party. I'm working seven days now just to get back all the money I've lost through taking drugs.

"I've given up because of the expense and because of how much my body has been stuffed up. I'm heaps slower. I can tell when I'm talking that my tongue doesn't move as easily as it used to do. I feel I'm talking weird.

"It was a stage with me. Anna's death stopped me completely but I was stopping anyway.

"It hurts me so much that she's dead. Thinking about her hurts more now than it did when it first happened. I don't see any of my friends any more. I don't want to go out. I drink but not to get drunk. Just a couple of beers with my family. That sort of thing.

"I went to a Catholic high school. We were told not to take drugs but we weren't given any information about the dangers of them or anything like that. If adults tell you these things you don't usually take much notice.

"What happened to Anna has stopped some people but a lot haven't stopped. They are still saying: 'It can't happen to me.' If it does happen to them, or to anyone, you can't really blame it on the dealers. The dealers are just trying to make money, like everyone. If a person decides to take a drug, it's that person's responsibility, sort of thing."

10

SARINE'S STORY

Sarine's name suits her well. A beautiful dark-haired Armenian girl, she has eyes as black and sad as night. She is calm, composed and careful to find the right words to describe the way things were when she and Anna were friends.

Sarine, seventeen, was the fifth member of the tightly-knit group which self-destructed after that fateful weekend in October 1995. She describes herself as being older and wiser than the others; she has never used drugs.

"Anna was my true best friend.

"In the beginning it was Anna, Kathie, Eddie and me. Then Eddie left and there were just the three of us until Alexia and Chloe came along.

"We told each other everything about our lives but I was closer to Anna than the others. I shared more of my secrets and thoughts with her. She felt the same way about me. If she was down and depressed she would tell me and we would try to come up with a solution.

"Anna wasn't often depressed; she was jumping around and happy most of the time.

"We were five very different people in that group and naturally there were fights. They were usually about silly little things that weren't even important – you know how teenagers are. But Anna and I never had a fight or an argument. We were more alike than the others. She was very caring and she was always there for me. She came to my house with me every day. She had so much love. She never judged people. She was friendly and open and never ever bitchy.

"Anna was smart. She could have been clever at school but she didn't try very hard.

"The only problems Anna really had were because she wouldn't think before she did anything. She would say something or do something and only think about it afterwards when she found herself in trouble. She was completely different with me, but with the others she was always getting involved, jumping into every fight they had.

"I have been very restricted in the way I have been brought up. My parents have never let me do the things a lot of other girls my age do. Now I can see that it's better like this. It's enough to be a child and to have your parents tell you what is good and what is bad for you.

"I can see what has happened to my friends.

"If you give a fourteen-year-old illegal drugs there's going to be trouble. None of them think. None of that group ever considered what might happen to them.

"I know how Anna would have reacted on that night. She would have made a quick decision without thinking it through.

"I am so against drugs. I always have been. At first when they talked in front of me about what they were planning to do I would say: 'No, don't do that,' but after a while they stopped talking about it when I was there. They knew I hated it and they didn't want to upset me.

"It is so stupid – to get 'high' for two hours and then feel terrible afterwards and then to say they wished they hadn't done it.

"They start with cigarettes, then marijuana and then they go on to acid and other things. I saw one girl go crazy on drugs. Afterwards they say they wish they were straight, but they don't mean it. They like the feeling.

"When you're young, like us, you don't get told things, that's the trouble. I was always the oldest and wisest one in our group but I still didn't know enough.

"I didn't know enough to stop Anna."

11

ECSTASY

"In my youth," Father William replied to his son,
"I feared it might injure the brain;
But now that I'm perfectly sure I have none,
Why, I do it again and again."
(*Alice in Wonderland*, Lewis Carroll)

"Mum, bring me an ashtray," called Alexia, fifteen going on fifty, flopping onto the couch. "I'm dying for a smoke."

"Get me a beer, would you luv?" sighed Tony, forty-nine, work-weary and wishing he was still twenty-one. "I'm dying for a drink."

"I'm having the best night of my life!" gibbered Anna, just fifteen years and five months old. She would never get any older. She was dying of ecstasy.

Anna Wood was a healthy fifteen-year-old with no medical problems until she swallowed a "roundish oblong" of MDMA and washed it down with a swig of water in a dark Sydney street on 21 October 1995. The so-called ecstasy she expected enveloped her for four hours but as dawn broke she became ill. Within a few hours and without any medical treatment, she was in a coma. She never regained consciousness. Three days later she was dead.

One of the most controversial issues which was splashed out in the wave of publicity that rushed across the country in the wake of Anna's death was the actual cause of her death. Why, on that particular night, didn't it kill anyone else?

Was it ecstasy? Or was it the effects the ecstasy tablet produced?

The obvious question is: what's the difference?

The less than obvious answer is that ecstasy produces different effects in different people. These effects are influenced by the size and weight of the person, the amount taken, the person's mood, the circumstances in which the drug is taken, what the person does while the drug is acting on his or her body and whether other drugs have been taken as well.

According to her friends and witnesses, the only drug that Anna took that night was an ecstasy tablet. (Traces of cannabis were found in her blood, but these were so faint that they could have been absorbed passively or may have been the result of Anna smoking marijuana three or four weeks before her death.)

WHAT KILLED ANNA WOOD?

The precise way in which ecstasy killed Anna Wood was still being investigated when this book went to press. We have already seen how even small amounts of ecstasy affect different people in different ways.

There is no doubt that the poisonous chemical, MDMA, would have changed the way messages were carried to and from Anna's brain. Here is the most likely medical explanation of what happened after she took the ecstasy tablet.

The MDMA in the tablet Anna Wood took travelled in her bloodstream to the pituitary gland in her brain. The pituitary gland controls most of the major hormones in the body.

The toxic nature of the MDMA, to use a common teenage term, stuffed up the pituitary gland. It caused inappropriate secretions of Anna's anti-diuretic hormone (ADH) and this stopped her kidneys from working properly.

Normally the kidneys are very powerful organs; as much fluid as you pour in, they can pour out again. In other words, even if you drink an enormous amount, the kidneys cause you to urinate and out most of it comes. You would probably have to drink more than 20 litres before your kidney function was affected.

If the pituitary gland is working normally, the anti-diuretic hormone regulates the sodium level of the water passing through the kidneys.

Sodium is very important to the body. Most of the body's metabolic processes depend on there being a normal concentration of sodium in the bloodstream. The level of sodium in the bloodstream determines how much water the body needs.

In Anna's case, the poison in the pituitary gland affected the anti-diuretic hormone, which in turn produced an increase in the sodium level of Anna's urine. This meant the urine became very concentrated and at the same time, the sodium level in Anna's blood decreased.

This increase in sodium in the urine and consequent drop in sodium in the blood could also have been caused by Anna taking excessive exercise and drinking heaps of water, although this is unlikely as she would have needed to drink a great deal of water for that to happen – as stated already, about 20 litres. She would hardly have had time to spend on the dance floor at all!

It is possible that Anna suffered from a combination of both the malfunctioning pituitary gland and the consumption of too much water.

Owing to the remarkable mechanics of the human body, the pressure in the blood vessels must always be equal to that of the surrounding cells. This is called osmotic pressure. If the sodium level in the blood decreases, osmotic pressure will cause the body's supply of water to flow out of the blood vessels and into the adjacent cells and also into the interstitial space (the area between the blood vessels and the cells).

This condition is called hyponatraemia. It has been described as drowning from the inside.

The opposite case is when you lose fluid from the body; water then moves from the cells *into* the bloodstream, to keep osmotic pressure even. This is more common and is called dehydration.

Because she had hyponatraemia, Anna's brain cells started to swell. There was nowhere else for all that water to go.

It is particularly dangerous for the brain to increase in size, because there is so little room inside the skull for expansion.

As her brain swelled more and more from the pressure of the water in the cells, Anna would have had nausea, vomiting, confusion – and obviously headache, although she apparently did not complain of head pain while she was still conscious.

Anna's brain swelled so much that the lower end or stem was forced down through the hole in the base of the skull where the spinal cord joins the brain. This hole is called the foramen magnum.

The brain stem contains the body's respiratory drive. Once it was pushed down through the foramen magnum, the mechanics of respiration would have stopped working. Normal breathing would have stopped. This is called respiratory arrest.

When respiration (breathing) stopped, oxygen was no longer being sent to the brain and the result was acute brain injury or hypoxic encephalopathy. This was the cause of death given in the original coroner's report.

Even medical specialists cannot always work out if a person has had acute hypoxic brain damage. When Anna triggered the ventilator at the hospital herself on the day after she was admitted to Intensive Care, there was a remote chance that she could still somehow breathe on her own. However, this flicker of improvement was not sustained and within a few hours it became clear that no oxygen at all was getting through to Anna's brain. The medical term to describe her condition at that stage is brain dead.

Anna's other organs continued to work with assistance of machines, which is the reason why they were healthy enough for donation.

Similar cases have occurred in Britain, where relatively low doses of MDMA combined with large quantities of water have been associated with hyponatraemia and water intoxication.

The main message from the cause of Anna Wood's death is that while the tablet she took may not have been *highly* poisonous, it triggered a malfunction in her brain which killed her.

WHAT IS ECSTASY?

Ecstasy used to be a lovely word. It means joy, rapture, unqualified delight. Now that it has become the name of a drug, people who say they are dying of ecstasy are right. But it's not joy which is killing them.

"Ecstasy" is a drug which causes stimulation and hallucination to a highly abnormal degree. Its real name is MethyleneDioxyMethAmphetamine or MDMA – the name of the chemical from which it is made. It is sold as a small white or yellow tablet, round or oval in shape and a little thicker than a Panadol tablet. It is usually taken by mouth and tastes terrible. Some people have been known to inject themselves with MDMA.

Ecstasy is sometimes referred to as XTC, Adam, Es, Essence, Clarity, Eccies or X.

The chemical structure of MDMA is similar to the structure of amphetamines ("speed") and some hallucinogens. Amphetamines are stimulants. They directly affect the central nervous system by speeding up the activity of certain chemicals in the brain.

Hallucinogens are drugs which can cause hallucinations – which means seeing, hearing, feeling or smelling things that do not exist. Other hallucinogens include LSD.

MDMA was developed in 1914 by a German chemical company for use as an appetite suppressant. Later, in the 1970s, it was used by psychotherapists in the United States as a "mood modifier". In 1985 its clinical use was banned because of its capacity to cause brain damage and its potential for misuse.

It has been available on the illegal drug market in Australia since about 1980 and, despite its previous history, has been wrongly promoted as a "safe" drug. In the 1993 National Drug Strategy household survey, 3 per cent of Australians said they had taken MDMA at some time in their lives and 1 per cent said they had used it within the last twelve months. Ecstasy is especially popular within the homosexual community.

Ecstasy is strongly associated with dance parties, known in the nineties as "raves", where its stimulating effects, while putting the users' health at risk, make it possible for them to move strenuously for hours at a time.

WHAT DOES ECSTASY DO?
The immediate effects can begin within an hour of taking ecstasy and usually last for up to six hours, but some may persist for up to thirty-two hours.

Ecstasy induces a feeling of intense wellbeing and closeness to others. It increases confidence and creates enormous amounts of energy. Ecstasy supposedly enhances "intuitive powers", making even the most trivial conversation appear deep and meaningful. It is said to enhance sexuality, although there is no evidence that MDMA improves sexual performance.

Conversely, ecstasy increases pulse rate and blood pressure and causes sweating, dehydration, jaw-clenching, grinding teeth, nausea, flickering vision, loss of appetite, anxiety and paranoia (fear of persecution or feelings of superiority).

A stronger reaction or a higher dose can produce hallucinations, such as moving floors and furniture, sensations of floating, irrational behaviour, panic attacks, convulsions (fits) and vomiting.

Because ecstasy is usually taken by people who are dancing vigorously in a hot and crowded environment, dehydration and a decreased ability to perspire may contribute to hyperthermia. This means that the body overheats; hyperthermia has been a common cause in ecstasy-related illness and deaths in Britain.

One symptom of hyperthermia is overwhelming thirst and the desire to drink extraordinary amounts of water. This in itself can be fatal.

The hangover effects the day after the drug is taken include fatigue, loss of appetite, insomnia, depression, muscle aches and problems with concentration.

While "coming down" there are likely to be muscle spasms, teeth-grinding and jaw tension, and in some people the symptoms of flu.

Because the unpleasant effects of the drug soon start to outweigh the pleasurable feelings that ecstasy produces, few people stay with it. Research suggests that, with prolonged use, the positive effects diminish while the negative effects increase, hangovers and burnout lasting longer and longer with each dose.

Nobody knows what the long-term effects of ecstasy are. There has been little research – it's only been widely available since 1988 – but evidence suggests that after protracted use, brain cells are damaged. Former users can suffer from prolonged depression.

New research in the United Kingdom released in February 1996, has shown that long-term use of ecstasy causes major damage to the liver, heart and brain. A research team from Sheffield University held post-mortem examinations of seven young British men who had died after taking ecstasy and the results ranged from swelling, bleeding and damaged nerves in the brain, to massive heart damage, striking changes in the livers and internal bleeding in the lungs.

People who take more than the occasional tablet, two or three or even more in a night, are running a much greater risk of getting very serious negative effects.

HOW DOES ECSTASY WORK?

Even doctors admit they don't know yet how ecstasy works. It's believed that MDMA may affect the way the brain handles serotonin, which is a natural chemical in the human body used to transmit messages of pleasure and happiness.

Some experiments with rats indicated that MDMA has an influence on the release of serotonin and, to a lesser degree, of another brain chemical called dopamine. However, nobody knows how far that influence goes. Prescribed drugs, such as appetite suppressants, also cause the release of serotonin without having the same effect on the body as MDMA.

Nor are there enough clues to the mystery of why one person will die after taking ecstasy while that person's group of friends, who have all taken ecstasy from the same source, will recover.

After the death of Anna Wood, the New South Wales Deputy State Coroner, Mr John Abernethy, commented that even the country's leading forensic pathologists and toxicologists knew little about the effects produced by ecstasy and were working hard to build up a bank of information so that further deaths could be prevented. Because of the variation in the way ecstasy affected different people, this was a difficult task which could not be achieved overnight.

MDMA is regarded as particularly dangerous for people with medical conditions such as heart or breathing problems and for people with depression or any other psychological disorder.

WHO IS DYING?

"You can't just say that Anna Wood died of ecstasy," said Paul Dillon, Information Officer for the University of New South Wales National Drug and Alcohol Research Centre. "Anna died from complications *resulting* from taking ecstasy.

"It's the same with AIDS. People don't die of AIDS. They die of illnesses related to having the AIDS virus in their system.

"It's like alcohol. Many people who are killed by alcohol are not necessarily killed by the drink itself. They are killed in car accidents, domestic violence, street brawls – they die from complications resulting from drinking alcohol."

Between February and December 1995, in Australia, there were five reported deaths from complications after taking ecstasy. By mid-March 1996, ecstasy had taken two more lives.

A spokesman for the Australian Government Analytical Laboratories, which investigates the content of illicit drugs seized during efforts to import them into the country, said it's the pure ecstasy in the tablets which has the greatest capacity to kill or cause brain damage.

"People say it's a terrible thing that backyard chemists are putting other chemicals into the drugs," said one laboratory chemist. "So it is. But it is the toxicity [poison] of the ecstasy itself that is the most terrible thing. It gives kids a high but it can also kill them, as it has done in the last twelve months. There are also people in hospitals ten years after taking ecstasy and other amphetamines who have still not recovered."

Also highly dangerous is the fact that nobody has any way of knowing what they are getting when they buy a tablet. Because the drug is not manufactured by a pharmaceutical company, nobody has any idea what quantity of MDMA the tablet contains or what the effects of that dose will be.

The same applies to other illegal drugs, like amphetamines. The manufacture of derivatives from amphetamines is increasing every year. There used to be only a couple on the illegal market; now there are at least ten being sold. Some are professionally produced; others are trial and error jobs which are often botched.

While it is not in the manufacturers' interests to mix their product with such poisonous substances as household cleaners, anaesthetics, cosmetics and even rat killer (as has been claimed in press reports), the reality is that when it comes to making drugs, there are no rules and no controls. Big-time drug operators have access to all the chemicals they need. The backyard chemists who make their version of ecstasy have difficulty getting the ingredients essential for making pure MDMA and must rely on making do with other chemicals.

"One theory," said Paul Dillon, "is that they try to match the usual ingredients instead, introducing chemicals which create poisonous drugs. Ecstasy is a chemical concoction and nobody knows what's really in it or what it does.

"This could explain why there were no reported deaths from ecstasy between 1988, when it was introduced into this country, and early 1995."

Another reason for the sudden leap in ecstasy-related deaths could be that more people are now using ecstasy. Or perhaps many of the deaths in the last decade which were attributed to accidents or suicide were actually the result of complications relating to ecstasy.

In the United Kingdom, since 1990, fifty-two ecstasy-related deaths have been reported in a country where, according to Paul Dillon, half a million ecstasy users swallow three million tablets every weekend. The ratio of risks to deaths seems small, but the death of an eighteen-year-old, Leah Betts, who took an ecstasy tablet at her own birthday party and died in November 1995, caused outrage similar to the community howl of pain that followed Anna Wood's death.

As long ago as 1991, British doctors working in the National Poisons Unit at Guy's Hospital in London noted that there was a striking increase in the number of calls concerning the misuse of MDMA.

After investigating the ecstasy-related deaths of seven young people in England (aged from sixteen to twenty-one) and four others who recovered after extensive hospital treatment, doctors warned that the increase in cases of toxicity due to MDMA and drugs sold as ecstasy deserved to be widely publicised. The British doctors stated that the serious adverse side effects which ecstasy was capable of causing exploded claims that it was a "safe" drug.

TEENAGERS AND ECSTASY
According to the Commonwealth Department of Human Services and Health statistics on drug abuse in Australia, issued

in 1994, 3 per cent of the whole population had tried ecstasy or designer drugs. Five per cent of males aged fourteen to twenty-four had taken ecstasy. Nine per cent of women in the same age group had tried it.

Ecstasy particularly appeals to young women because it doesn't have the same effect on them as alcohol. "They can take it believing that it doesn't affect their appearance," said Paul Dillon. "They can dance for hours and feel good about themselves."

Young men, on the other hand, just go out and get drunk.

"The females who use ecstasy aren't usually kids," says Paul Dillon. "They are usually young single women with high disposable incomes and an 'inner city' attitude – whether or not they actually live there. They believe it's 'cool' to use 'recreational drugs' like ecstasy.

"For most adult ecstasy users, it's their drug of choice. They don't normally indulge in other drugs.

"The vast majority of teenage kids will not take ecstasy. They don't have that sort of money. However, we have to tell them the truth.

"If you claim that ecstasy is a deadly drug which will kill them the minute they use it, they will know you're wrong and anything you tell them about drugs will lose credibility.

"The more adults say that ecstasy and the designer drugs are killers, that they are awful, they're terrible, the more kids will look around and see other kids taking them and nothing happening to them, nothing at all. Their friends are going out at the weekend and putting God knows what into their bodies and coming back to school on Monday looking fine.

"The inevitable conclusion they will come to is that somebody's lying to them.

"Kids need to know that all drugs are harmful, but some drugs are more dangerous than others. They also need to know that if they or their friends take drugs and become ill, they must get medical help."

Getting help fast!

As soon as anyone who has taken ecstasy or any illegal drug becomes ill, an ambulance should be called. Getting to the nearest hospital is a top priority. There will be no legal action or reprisals taken by the ambulance or hospital staff against the victims of drug abuse or the people who bring them for treatment.

If you are with a friend who is not behaving normally, who is not happy with the effects he or she is experiencing, get help.

Even if you are not ill, if you have taken something and you don't like the feeling . . . if you feel uncomfortable or out of control . . . if you don't want to be where you are . . . if you feel frightened or worried about what is happening to you . . . GET MEDICAL HELP.

Ask someone to take you to a doctor, hospital or medical centre.

Get the people with you to call an ambulance. Tell the medical officers what you have had, how much and when you had it.

Don't imagine that the sickness will just go away and you'll feel better in the morning.

That's what Anna Wood and her friends did.

Don't waste time apologising for making a fool of yourself.

You could die of embarrassment.

12

WICKED RISKS

In another moment down went Alice after it,
never once considering how in the world
she was to get out again.
(*Alice in Wonderland*, Lewis Carroll)

All her life Anna Wood was lucky. She was adored by her
parents, well cared for, lovely to look at; she had travelled, she
was cheerful, intelligent, healthy, articulate, confident and loved
by everyone who knew her.

Like most fifteen-year-olds, she took risks. Now and then
she had a drink or a smoke. She puffed a marijuana cigarette
with her sister and occasionally with her friends. She probably
experimented once with speed, but the effect apparently
frightened her sufficiently into returning to her previous anti-
drug stance.

For Anna it was an enormous risk to wag school one day
in order to set out on an anti-drug mission. Again she was
lucky. The principal knew her mother, who was involved in
various school activities. He rang Angela Wood at work, and
she came to the school to nip any further forays into truancy
in the bud.

Angela was not surprised when the principal phoned. She had
just taken a call from Anna herself, who was so overwhelmed

with guilt at skipping classes that she had rung her mother to confess what she had done.

According to a student at Anna's school, she would not have been the only student absent that day because of drugs.

"Most of the kids who do drugs take them in the morning before school," said the boy. "Then they stay away all day so that when it's time to go home in the afternoon, the effects have worn off.

"They get the stuff from people around the shopping centre, either after school so they can take it next morning, or early in the morning, when their parents think they're already at school."

Anna Wood knew about this practice.

The day that she found herself in trouble for wagging school, she was accompanying her friend Chloe on a visit to the girl who regularly supplied Chloe with cannabis. "Chloe was so involved in the drug scene she didn't know how to get out of it," said a friend of both girls. "Once they know you're hooked they won't let you out. Anna was so angry about what drugs were doing to Chloe, she went with her to tell these older kids to leave Chloe alone."

This was the sort of risk that appealed to Anna, the champion of the underdog – a confrontation with evil (albeit pretty small-time evil) to rescue a maiden who was being seduced by wicked promises of unreal joy.

Yet instead of saving her friend, a few months later Anna herself was seduced by the magic of the wicked risk – and on 21 October 1995, Anna Wood's lifetime of luck ran out.

"Anna Wood was about as unlucky as it's possible to be," said Dr Simon Clarke, a consultant physician in adolescent medicine at Westmead Hospital in Sydney.

"Kids are out getting blind drunk every night of the week and most of them don't get killed. Hundreds of people are taking ecstasy every weekend and they're not all dying.

"These days, a lot of drunken kids are saved from death by the drink driving laws. Illegal drugs, naturally, are not governed by such laws. Drugs are made by morons who only have to get one radical wrong in the mix to produce poisons which may result in death or permanent brain damage. Nobody knows what's in them. Nobody knows what they might do.

"Anna Wood took the same risk that thousands of other teenagers do. She had been out dancing before. She would have seen people all around her, high on ecstasy and apparently having a marvellous time. How could she have known what a dangerous game she was playing?"

WHY KIDS TAKE CHANCES

Needless to say, some kids take bigger risks than others. But one way or another, almost all adolescents do it. They have to take risks to win the respect of their peers, to prove they are mature, to break through the safety barrier which parents have erected around them since the day they were born.

Some kids skydive. Some abseil from rocks in remote bush. Some take boards out into an unguarded ocean and pit themselves against the waves.

Some play football – in terms of potential injury, probably the silliest thing they can do; in terms of the glory they can achieve, a risk worth taking.

Some go out onto a concert stage and risk failure.

Some run away from home – and risk not being found.

Some take drugs – and risk death.

Taking risks is a natural part of growing up. Breaking down the barriers of childhood, doing things they've never done before, going places they've never been – this is all part of the process that's involved in establishing themselves as independent individuals.

Almost all teenagers long for new experiences. Within reason, and despite their inevitable anxiety, most parents wouldn't want it any other way.

Dr David Bennett, Head of Adolescent Medicine at the Royal Alexandra Hospital for Children in Sydney, said it was natural for a majority of young people to want to try out new skills, to test the limits of their abilities, to compete, to challenge, to rebel.

"Kids who are in the frenzied grip of pubertal hormones, who are bursting at the seams with energy, are usually very impulsive when it comes to looking for thrills," said Dr Bennett.

"They often do things on the spur of the moment, with little thought for the consequences. In fact, it's not necessarily true that they don't care about what might happen. The truth is that they don't *know* what might happen. They are too immature to think things through the way adults do.

"Too many adolescents have not received adequate information about dangerous risks, such as taking drugs and drinking. They simply don't know enough about it."

For many reasons, adolescents, more than any other group, are likely to believe they are immortal – that "it", whatever "it" may be, won't happen to them.

You can't just talk them out of doing silly, impractical, dangerous and life-threatening things. Parents are no longer the only influence on their lives. For better or worse, the peer group and the community shape their behaviour and their beliefs.

"Our society teaches that sex, alcohol and purchasing power lead to the good life," said David Bennett. "So why should we be surprised that teenagers are the only age group whose health status has not improved in the past forty years?"

In fact, Dr Bennett believes there are clear indications that the health of adolescents in our society is deteriorating. Drug and alcohol abuse, depression and suicide, violent crime, eating disorders, and unsafe sexual behaviour occur with depressing regularity and at enormous cost to the community.

RISK EDUCATION

Risk-taking, as well as drug use and abuse, is covered in the Personal Development, Health and Physical Education curriculum (PD/Health/PE) which is taught in New South Wales high schools. The curriculum was devised by the New South Wales Board of Studies in co-operation with the departments of School Education and Health, with input from parent groups and private interest groups such as the Cancer Council and the anti-smoking lobby. The PD/Health/PE course has been mandatory in all government and non-government schools in New South Wales since 1992.

Students in Years Seven to Ten are required to participate in the course for 300 hours over four years – usually three forty-minute periods a week. Students in Years Eleven and Twelve do an intensive course over twenty-five hours, often in the form of a camp or seminar.

Most of Anna Wood's friends claimed that PD/Health lessons at their school had taught them nothing constructive about drugs. However, during three periods a week in Years Seven and Eight, four periods a week in Year Nine and two periods a week in Year Ten, Anna and her friends would have been present at discussions covering healthy living – fitness, nutrition, safe living practices, decision-making, skills development and self-esteem. Various parts of the course involved drugs and drug abuse. According to one teacher: "Some students choose to close their ears to the education they are given concerning drugs as it contradicts what they hear on the streets."

However, Eleanor Davidson, Director of Student Welfare for the New South Wales Department of School Education, agreed that specific information about illicit drugs would not have been provided to Anna Wood and her fellow students.

"Providing explicit facts had been tried in previous years and had proved to be inappropriate," said Ms Davidson. "We found that for some students, giving them information alone was like issuing them with a handbook on how to get into illegal drugs."

Ms Davidson said schools varied enormously in the way they presented the PD/Health course and the wide variation in the response from students reflected the fact that, for many, the message was still not getting through. Their experience outside school made Personal Development and Health a very difficult subject to teach.

"An enormous amount of work is going into ways of finding effective programs which will really help kids when it comes to coping with life," she said. "We are working with the Health Department and other health organisations, as well as parents. If parents know what the school is doing, they can build on that at home."

THE BEST AND WORST OF RISKS

There are two types of risk – dangerous risks and safe risks. The difference between abseiling and taking drugs is that one is a safe risk, where the danger can be controlled. The other is a dangerous risk, where the person taking the drug has no genuine way of knowing what he or she is putting into their body and what the result – both in the short and long term – may be.

According to Simon Clarke, unsafe risks are determined by a child's peer group. "They are usually the prerogative of teenagers who are less influenced by their family, school, church or community. For street kids, who have no structure for sensible risk-taking, the most readily available risks are those involving sex, drugs and breaking the law.

"Then there are children in crisis. These are the kids who are more likely to take dangerous risks. Children who are depressed over divorce and the breaking up of their family, who are anxious about their sexuality, who have low self-esteem from tragic childhood experiences or from struggling at school, who are worried about getting a job, who are suffering from a broken relationship of their own – these are the ones who will often gamble unwisely with their lives."

Anna Wood did not fit into either of these categories, yet the seeds of risk-taking had still been sown into fertile young soil.

"Anna Wood sounds as if she may have been typical of many fifteen-year-old Australian girls," said Dr Clarke. "She apparently played no regular sport – her only regular exercise was walking around the local mall. So taking a risk in some sporting or physical field was probably not an option.

"It's unfortunate that so many kids – especially girls – in this age group give up sport, as it not only enables them to take risks, it can also provide the self-esteem that success in organised recreational activities can bring. They give it up just when they need it most."

Anna joined a youth theatre group, and took risks there, unfortunately not all of the safe variety. She experimented with marijuana. Well, why not? Everybody else was doing it too.

Anna was not an academic – she was evidently concerned that her school results were not satisfying her parents, but not motivated enough to take on the challenge of excelling at school.

"She was also younger than her friends," said Dr Clarke. "Her birthday was in May, which means that like many children who start school before the age of five, she would have been almost a year younger than some of her classmates. As a result, it's quite possible her self-esteem was not as high as everyone believed.

"If we gave people marks for their social skills," said Dr Clarke, "Anna could have been top of the class and she might have felt a lot better about herself as well. From what we have been told about her, Anna's real gift was her ability to get on with people, her warmth, her success in convincing others that she cared about them.

"It has always seemed unfair to me that we commend kids on their science and maths skills but we never reward those with outstanding people skills."

RISKS BELONG AT HOME

Risk-taking, like charity, should begin at home. For teenagers in secure families, the "best risk" is to revolt against the family – to be a ratbag at home, to accuse their parents of not understanding them, to stay out late, to refuse to clean their rooms, to argue with everything – but in most cases, to succumb to grudging obedience.

Unfortunately, not all children in functional and apparently loving families feel as secure as their parents believe. This is possibly the result of the breathtaking pressure of work and time which is currently afflicting working families everywhere.

The point is that teenagers can't impress their parents with their risk-taking, shock them with their new skills, and make them angry with their stupid behaviour, ugly clothes and toilet-brush haircuts, unless the parents are there. If there is nobody at home, they are more likely to take risks to impress their peers – with all the dangers that can involve.

"Too many children in the thirteen to eighteen age group are simply not thought about or catered for in our society at all," said Dr Clarke, "so a lot of them get together and impress each other (rather than us) with their risk-taking. They smoke, they drink illegally, they take illicit drugs, they have unsafe sex."

Dr Clarke believes it is as important to be at home with teenage children as it is to be with infants. "The nurturing a mother provides to her baby is probably the most important thing she will do in her life," he said, "but people assume that because their adolescents are physically independent, they no longer need to do any parenting. They are so wrong.

"An empty house is lonely. Even adults know how hard it is to sit down and read or study when there is nobody else around to be interested in the effort you're making.

"Human beings are social animals. We need warmth; we need people around us. It's a matter of being organised. Somebody should be there for teenage kids when they get home from school – whether it's mum or dad doing it in shifts, or granny or aunty, or a family friend, a minder, or even a retired pensioner who is looking for an interest."

Of course, many families *are* doing the right thing by their adolescent children. It's quite possible that even the most devoted and caring parents, who are making huge sacrifices to be around, organised and available when their teenagers need them, will still be stunned by the silly risks their children decide to take. To that neither the professionals nor the parents can come up with an answer.

However, it does seem that people are opting out of parenting earlier than they used to. It's not a good idea. You have to be around for your teenagers not only to build them up and provide security, but so they can break away. You have to be there to run the family, but your presence is also essential so that they can criticise your old-fashioned views, your sensible clothes, your political bias, your bland music, the way you pull your socks up instead of squashing them down and the ridiculous things that interest you, like fine china or smelly books or garden grubs. They must have something to break away from, even if it's just your obsession with the toilet seat and matching clothes and wearing singlets and eating apples – anything that typifies the whole boring, tedious life you lead, the sort of life from which they will one day escape.

In the meantime, you have to be stable so they can be erratic. You have to be there so that they can yell at you and blame you and hold you responsible for their skin, their bad hair days, their marks, their poverty and their crippled social life.

"The expression 'I spend quality time with my children'," said Dr Clarke, "is as big a lie as 'Of course I'll still love you in the morning', 'The cheque's in the post' and 'I'm from the government, I'm here to help you'.

"You don't have to spend quality time with your adolescent children. You just have to spend time with them."

Don't panic. This advice doesn't necessarily mean parents have to hang around in the same room as their teenagers, they don't have to stare into their eyes and have in-depth debates with them about the state of the world.

You do have to touch them, Dr Clarke said. "They usually appreciate a hug more than you'd suspect. You do have to tell them how much you care about them – they need to know, even though the reply will probably be: 'Oh you're just my father/mother; you have to say that'."

Most of all, you just have to be there.

How can your teenagers rebel if you're not there to notice?

How can they discard you if you have already discarded them?

13

DRINKING, SMOKING, CHOOFING

However, this bottle was *not* marked "poison", so Alice ventured to
taste it, and finding it very nice . . . she very soon finished it off.
"What a curious feeling!" said Alice.
(*Alice in Wonderland*, Lewis Carroll)

After watching her mum and dad run a pub for four years, Anna
Wood wasn't even slightly excited by the thought of getting
drunk. To Anna and her sister Alice, alcohol was associated with
warmth, shelter, food, music and the company of good friends.
In this, the girls were exceptions to the general rule.

For a vast majority of teenagers, the most popular drug in
Australia is alcohol. Correspondingly, in the short term, more
young lives are lost due to alcohol consumption (mostly through
road accidents) than any other single cause.

In the longer term the biggest killer drug is tobacco. Despite
the fact that alcohol and nicotine both have a horrifying effect
on health, cigarettes and drink are not illegal for adults, so
teenagers presume they present a relatively safe risk. Even most
parents are resigned to the idea that kids will inevitably "break
out" by having a drink.

To suggest in the 1990s that this attitude is irresponsible is to
invite contradiction and controversy. Certainly, people who don't
drink alcohol are as healthy, happy and as capable of relaxing

and enjoying themselves as people who tipple. However, the consumption of alcohol has been part of our culture for thousands of years – since longer ago than Jesus had to rescue the wedding feast when it ran out of wine. Drinking with meals, drinking in the company of family and friends, drinking in celebration, has been part of the human lifestyle since life on earth began.

The main difference between drinking in moderation and taking illicit drugs is that drugs are generally consumed purely for the abnormal effects they produce. They are not taken in celebration, they are not taken to rejoice. True, some drugs, such as marijuana and ecstasy, are usually consumed in a group environment and the illicit nature of the deed unites people in a titillating sense of togetherness. However, the main reason most drugs are taken is for the synthetic emotional, mental and physical feelings they create.

The abuse of alcohol – drinking to excess purely for the sake of blocking out reality – has a similar effect and is done for the same reason as taking illegal drugs. Binge drinking is deadly. It kills many more of our young people than drugs do, because it's easier to get, more of them do it and it's just as dangerous.

"Australia's attitude to alcohol is unique in the world," said Paul Dillon, from the University of New South Wales National Drug and Alcohol Research Centre. "Because of the culture in which they've been brought up, kids here drink to get drunk."

Australia is in the world's top twenty countries when it comes to alcohol consumption – for beer drinking, we have made it into the top ten! Not surprisingly, alcohol-related illness is the fourth major health problem in the country, closely following heart disease, cancer and mental illness.

"The same weekend that Anna Wood died, there were newspaper reports of six youths dying from alcohol-related injuries," said Mr Dillon. "They only rated a few lines of type, because that sort of death is so depressingly common. Yet Anna's death was still making national headlines a month after she died."

GROG

From their early teens, young people are conditioned to believe that you can't relax and have a good time without a drink in your hand. In the nineties they drink twice as much as they did twenty years ago. Often they begin with spirits – rum, whisky and vodka – because the biting, burning, unpleasant taste can be improved by adding soft drinks. It's a bit like washing down nasty medicine with something sweet. After all, when they were small they were given medicine to make them feel better. Not enough of them understand the difference.

The New South Wales and Victorian Health departments have introduced surveys every three years to monitor drug use among adolescents. The most recent statistics, from the 1993 New South Wales research (more will be acquired in 1996) suggest that although the number of school students in the twelve to sixteen age group who drink alcohol every week fell from around 64 per cent in 1989 to 35 per cent in 1992, those who binge drink are doing it in higher numbers.

The girls are doing it too, even as young as fourteen.

The older teenagers get, the more alcohol they consume, with the heaviest drinking occurring around sixteen and seventeen.

The 1995 National Drug Strategy household survey found that 44 per cent of fourteen- to nineteen-year-olds – 43 per cent boys, 33 per cent girls – had drunk five or more alcoholic drinks on their last drinking occasion.

Twenty per cent of teenagers (22 per cent of boys and 18 per cent of girls) drink regularly – at least once a week.

Generally, by the age of seventeen, boys are drinking beer, like every good Australian bloke, while girls are staying with the sweetly strong stuff.

The acute problems resulting from teenage drinking include drunkenness, violence, arrests and accidents. Dr David Bennett, who has written his own manual for parents – *Growing Pains: What to Do When Your Children Turn into Teenagers*, published by Doubleday – points out that these problems result from the fact that alcohol is a depressant, not a stimulant as many people think, and is dangerously intoxicating, especially to young people. "Teenage deaths from toxic overdose have usually involved a dare to down a bottle of spirits," said Dr Bennett. "For most young drivers, however, dangerous behaviour and drunk/drugged driving pose a greater threat to life. "Longer-term problems are less obvious. While no-one can say for sure whether or not teenage drinking patterns persist into adulthood, the earlier you start, and the heavier you drink, the earlier you get damaged. The details are depressing: cirrhosis of the liver, some cancers, chronic malnutrition and the risk of infection and, of course, brain damage."

Heavy drinking does shrink the brain. According to Dr Bennett, it causes an absolute loss of cortical tissue (reversible, fortunately, in young people who stop before it's too late).

Dr Simon Clarke says our society excludes kids from sensible drinking habits. He believes we have a lot to learn from Mediterranean countries, whose climate is similar enough to ours for us to follow their example.

"In Mediterranean countries there is a different attitude to alcohol," said Dr Clarke. "They have high alcohol consumption but a low record of alcoholism.

"We should all be drinking at our local tavernas, with our teenagers in tow.

"If we taught our children to drink wine in a moderate way and from an early age, it would teach them how to make alcohol part of their life without depending upon it for social success, in the way so many Australians do.

"If that was the way we enjoyed ourselves here, Anna Wood and her friends might not have had to go to raves to have fun."

In the less than ideal world of adolescent Australia in the nineties, however, the pressure to "be cool" is too strong for teenagers to mix happily with their peers under the eagle eyes of the parents.

Dr Bennett suggests that "Kids will always get together away from their parents, and do what they want to do, no matter what."

SMOKES

Tobacco is the biggest killer drug in Australia, followed by alcohol. Taken up in the teenage years, cigarette smoking is the greatest preventable threat to health and life. According to David Bennett, 30 per cent of all fatal cancers could be prevented by people not smoking.

Adults are taking notice. Only a third of Australia smokes today. Teenage smoking, however, is increasing.

In *Growing Pains* Dr Bennett writes:

> • the influence of close friends who smoke is the number one reason for starting;
> • a teenager is twice as likely to smoke if both parents smoke and four times as likely to smoke if parents and older siblings smoke.

Cigarettes contain nicotine, tar and other chemicals, some of which are toxic and forty-three of which have been identified as being carcinogenic – that is, they cause cancer. Carbon monoxide is found in tobacco smoke and is more concentrated in the lungs of people who smoke.

Nicotine is a poison. A few drops can kill an adult. In Australian-made cigarettes, the amount of nicotine is limited to 1.4 milligrams. Nicotine causes stimulation and then a feeling of relaxation. It causes the blood vessels to narrow, thereby affecting circulation and causing blood pressure to rise. Tar is the main cause of lung and throat cancer and aggravates bronchial and respiratory disease.

Thirteen per cent of teenagers smoke regularly (every day or most days) and 5 per cent smoke fewer than five cigarettes a day. Currently, girls smoke more than boys; smoking seems to have a link with sexual appeal, although only in the minds of the girls who do it. Cigarette consumption tends to increase with age.

The 1995 National Drug Strategy household survey also found just over half (57 per cent) of the fourteen- to nineteen-year-olds who had ever smoked a full cigarette don't smoke any more.

A survey of New South Wales primary school students aged ten to twelve indicated that only about 2 per cent smoked regularly, although 30 per cent of boys and 20 per cent of girls had actually tried a cigarette at some time in their lives. Children with family members and best friends who smoked and those getting five dollars or more in weekly pocket money were more likely to try smoking.

"Nobody, apart from kids themselves, should need any convincing that teenage smoking is a major health problem," said Dr Bennett. "The longer-term consequences in particular (a fifteen times greater chance of developing lung disease and lung cancer and an eight times greater chance of heart disease) are bad enough. However, teenagers who smoke soon develop a cough, produce phlegm and become short of breath on exertion, lose stamina, get a bad taste in the mouth, stains on their teeth and an unpleasant odour on their breath, fingers, hair and clothes. Smoke also irritates eyes, causes skin to wrinkle faster and hair to discolour, soon making smokers look older than their years."

Dr Bennett said he was concerned that many people didn't realise that nicotine is an extremely addictive drug. On the other hand, if a person under twenty-five is able to stop smoking, the health risks revert to normal and the side effects begin to improve within two or three weeks of giving up.

MARIJUANA

The most popular illicit drug – if you don't count tobacco and alcohol, drugs which are also illegal as far as children are concerned – is cannabis, also known as marijuana, dope, grass, weed, hooch, hash or pot.

This drug is based on the oil contained in the leaves and seeds of the Indian hemp plant, cannabis. Smoking the dried leaves and seed heads of the cannabis or marijuana plant produces feelings of intoxication and relaxation similar to the effects of alcohol.

Even though cannabis is illegal in all states, school children seem to have easy access to it. South Australia introduced an expiation policy for cannabis in 1987 and the Australian Capital Territory followed suit in 1992. Expiation is commonly referred to as decriminalisation; it means that people found using or in possession of small amounts of marijuana are usually fined on the spot rather than being charged with a criminal offence.

Police and health officials say it is difficult to find out whether expiation has caused an increase in the numbers of young people who smoke marijuana in South Australia as not enough large-scale surveys have been carried out. The statistics from small localised surveys vary a great deal and are influenced by many other factors.

For children who choose to experiment with drugs, there is a definite link between smoking cigarettes and smoking marijuana.

According to the 1995 National Drug Strategy, 41 per cent of teenagers aged from fourteen to nineteen had been offered marijuana in the previous twelve months, 35 per cent of those surveyed had smoked it at some time and 28 per cent had smoked it in the previous year.

A survey of Victorian and New South Wales secondary school students in September 1992 showed that 15 per cent in New South Wales and 13 per cent in Victoria had used marijuana in the previous four weeks. The same survey indicated that, apart from marijuana and inhalants, the use of illicit drugs was minimal.

Statistics suggest that most children who smoke marijuana do not tend to move on to harder drugs. On the other hand, the teenagers who knew Anna Wood well had all progressed from cigarettes to marijuana, and then to speed, LSD and ecstasy.

An associated problem is that because cannabis is illegal, its use can put young people in contact with drug dealers and criminals – or at the least, the "rough crowd" at school.

Marijuana is an intoxicant – it makes users feel relaxed and often a bit silly; it sometimes creates the impression that time is slowing down. It can also cause dryness in the mouth, red eyes, poor co-ordination, panic attacks, dizziness and increased appetite. Cannabis is not addictive in the same way as nicotine; however, while the effects of smoking a marijuana cigarette, joint or "bong" last for two to four hours, the drug remains in the system for much longer.

Marijuana is not only the drug chosen by teenagers. Since the sixties, when in their ignorance a generation of hippies took it up and made it their own, men and women of all ages, sometimes working in even the loftiest professions, have used cannabis. They justify smoking pot because it has always been seen as a "soft" drug which, unlike tobacco, has no long-term negative effects on health. Recent research, however, suggests that their information is wrong.

The National Drug Strategy's Cannabis Task Force has reported that if consumed frequently (on a weekly or daily basis), cannabis has as great a potential for harm as alcohol and tobacco. For example, evidence suggests that the tar content of cannabis is far greater than that of tobacco. Consequently, smoking even small quantities of cannabis could cause cancers and respiratory diseases similar to those experienced by chain smokers.

The risks of emotional and psychiatric disorders typically associated with the use of alcohol and other psychoactive drugs are equally applicable to cannabis, even more so if these drugs are used together.

The problem is that many people use marijuana without any obvious ill effects, so that the dangers of the drug are often underestimated.

In *Growing Pains*, Dr David Bennett says chronic marijuana users become very psychologically dependent and cannot or will not believe that it is causing them harm. "Other drawbacks include loss of energy and drive and impairment of short-term memory and concentration, effects that have been shown to persist long after people stop using the drug (and may not be reversible, suggesting physiological changes in the brain)."

Dr Bennett said heavy long-term marijuana use can also lead to symptoms of airways obstruction, and increases the risk (sixfold) of developing schizophrenia as well as cancer of the mouth, jaw, tongue and lung.

114

"Unlike other drugs of abuse, which are single chemicals (for example, alcohol, cocaine and LSD), marijuana contains 421 known chemicals, sixty-one of which are unique chemicals called cannabinoids (only a handful of which have been studied)."

Dr Bennett said cannabis accumulates in body fat and unlike alcohol is not washed quickly out of the body. It would take about a month for all the chemicals in a single joint to clear from the body.

"Unlike the cannabis in circulation decades ago, today's supplies have a higher content of delta–9-tetrahydro-cannabinol (THC), the cannabinoid most responsible for the 'high'."

Evidence is growing that marijuana can damage the lungs, heart, brain, immune system and reproductive organs. Of more immediate concern, however, is the fact that marijuana is just as dangerous to driving as alcohol. "It interferes with motor and co-ordination skills, vision and perception of time and space," said Dr Bennett. "So the combination of marijuana and alcohol is devastating to anyone taking the wheel of a car."

GETTING "COOL"

From the time children reach double figures the heat is on to be cool.

A research project carried out by Peta Odgers, from the Graduate School of Education at the University of Western Australia, has revealed that a great deal of teenage drug use is motivated by getting the right sort of reputation.

Her conclusions, resulting from a survey of more than 1200 metropolitan high school students, suggest they often choose to drink, smoke and use marijuana in order to be accepted by particular groups of friends.

"Breaking rules and laws is secondary to their desire to fit in with the peer group," said Dr Odgers. "Equally, if they decide they want to be in a group which doesn't use drugs, they'll throw the stuff out the window and walk away.

"Most of them don't see doing drugs as an act of rebellion against the system at all. In fact, in a way they are conforming – they are doing what is required to get accepted into the group of their choice."

According to Dr Odgers, taking drugs is like wearing certain kinds of clothes or opting for particular hairstyles. Kids do it to be acceptable, to belong to the group they believe is most desirable.

Among students surveyed, cigarette smoking was often the first step in substance (drug) use; children as young as ten had used tobacco in primary school. Some of the students surveyed admitted they had tried alcohol and marijuana in Year Six (aged about eleven). Other illicit drugs were not generally tried until the end of Year Eight in high school and were most commonly used in Years Nine and Ten.

Dr Odgers followed up her extensive survey with in-depth interviews with students in Years Nine to Twelve at a cross-section of Perth high schools. Contrary to popular belief, these students said illicit drugs, other than marijuana, were not generally considered "cool". Alcohol, cigarettes and marijuana were the most common drugs of choice for school students.

Some students said cigarette smoking was a waste of time. "You don't get a high from it and it just wrecks your lungs." Sniffing volatile substances was also unacceptable.

The main reason the students gave for using drugs, or for their peers using drugs, was "to get a reputation so that they'll be accepted by their friends or to just fit in". Other reasons included "because their friends did it", "just wanting to see what it was like" and "a bad family life or stress". These reasons did not vary much with the age of the students.

Dr Odgers found that alcohol and marijuana were social activities carried out when friends were all together; if they drank or smoked dope alone it was regarded by group members as the first sign of addiction.

With the exception of tobacco, students liked to share the costs as well as the experience of drug-taking with their friends. All drugs were most commonly acquired through friends and siblings; the exception was a few easily accessible retail outlets where alcohol and cigarettes could be purchased without difficulty. Holidays were the best time for drug indulgence, not only because the students had more time to get what they wanted but because there was less parental supervision and more parties and they could sleep in the next morning without having to worry about going to school.

The most common reason given for giving up drugs was because they "worked out what it was doing to their body". Other reasons included a bad experience – "like a bad trip or someone you know dies or something" – not being able to "handle it" and getting caught. The majority of students who used drugs said they would probably eventually stop taking all drugs except alcohol, which they thought they would continue to use in moderation.

One boy, who began drinking and smoking marijuana when he was twelve, in order to get into a particular group, has now given up cigarettes and dope (but not alcohol) and says using these drugs was "a ridiculous thing to do".

"If these supposed friends won't accept you for who you are then you should just forget them – you're better off on your own." He said giving up marijuana and cigarettes meant he had to change his group of friends.

Most of the students interviewed said it "wasn't worth it" if a group accepted them *only* if they used drugs; at the same time, the majority admitted that using drugs was the way to belong, to be popular, to get more friends and to acquire a "cool" reputation. Fourteen- and fifteen-year-old boys were the most susceptible to this sort of pressure.

The Western Australian students favoured scare tactics as the best method of drug education. Older students, in Years Eleven and Twelve, thought it was important to have the opportunity to talk with someone about the issues associated with drug use. This did not mean authority figures. Instead they suggested "someone who could relate to where high school kids were coming from and who had either been a part of the drug scene or at least understood what it was like".

Students felt it was vitally important for them to be given the opportunity to openly discuss their involvement, their fears and concerns and to be able to ask questions without fear of reprisals.

Not surprisingly, students' opinions of themselves varied depending on whether or not they used drugs. Those who didn't were happy to conform and to be law-abiding; they wanted to be known as good and friendly people who could be trusted and were popular among their peers. They were confident about their friendships and their social life and were particularly happy about their relationship with their families. They were positive and constructive in the way they dealt with the problems in their lives.

In contrast, students who used drugs were identified in the study as being less confident in themselves and believed they were less liked by their families. Their attitude to solving problems tended towards unrealistic hopes – for example, maybe a miracle might happen . . . Drug users didn't want to be seen as conformists, didn't admire pro-social activities (such as being a good athlete) and were more likely to strive to be mean, to cause trouble, break rules and be unreliable.

Students who had used drugs but had made the decision to give them up tended to fall between these two extremes. They wanted to conform, but not completely. The majority of these young people had stopped taking drugs in order to be accepted by a different social group and to develop a sense of belonging in a new circle of friends.

Dr Odgers said her report indicated the need for more appropriate, relevant and up-to-date drug education programs for adolescents. She suggested that the implementation of these programs should begin during primary school as almost 20 per cent of first year high school students were already involved in alcohol use and some children had begun smoking in primary school.

. . . AND PILLS

Legal painkillers which can be purchased at the chemist shop or even plucked from supermarket shelves are also drugs, even though they are not illicit ones. Health authorities are concerned at the fact that many children regularly take analgesics.

These days, nobody expects to have to put up with pain. Effective relief is just a tablet away – and while painkillers have a medicinal purpose, they can still be abused.

Children who become dependent on them are establishing life habits which will be hard to break. Relaxation, massage, a good night's sleep and a healthy diet can all contribute to pain relief without pharmaceutical drugs.

All it takes is time . . .

14

THE D-FILES

"Who am I then? Tell me that first, and then, if I like being that person, I'll come up: if not, I'll stay down here till I'm somebody else."
(*Alice in Wonderland*, Lewis Carroll)

The boy sat on his tractor, sniffing speed to stay awake. He had another field to plough before dark. In the village a few miles east, his young brother blew the money from his paper route on half a trip to LSD-land. In the city, after a long day at her new office, their sister swallowed ecstasy at a disco so she could keep on dancing long after her body begged her to stop.

Back home on the farm their mother read about Anna Wood and shook her head in disgust as she peeled a tub of potatoes. "That silly little girl was obviously spoilt and bored," she said to her husband. "Typical of city kids. Thank goodness ours have always been too hard-working and sensible to take drugs."

City kids, country kids. Kids from the suburbs, kids from the farms. Rich kids, poor kids, beggar kids, thieves. None is exempt from the temptations of the drug culture. Few of them realise the powerful influences which are at work to keep it flourishing. Not enough of them recognise the deadly risks it represents right now and also in the future that belongs to them.

The popular television show *The X-Files*, which has an enormous teenage following, is about investigations into the unknown.

Drugs come into that category. Not much is known about them, particularly the ones which have been classified as illegal.

"The scary thing about what has happened with marijuana is that it's been around for about thirty years with people saying it's harmless," said Paul Dillon, from the University of New South Wales National Alcohol and Drug Research Centre. "Now they know that isn't true.

"There are a lot of new 'designer' drugs available now. When they first come out people say the same thing about them. But who knows what we'll find out in the next ten or twenty years?"

For many users it will be too late to know. They will be like the millions of cigarette smokers who die every year. Back then, nobody told them what the drug would do to their bodies.

"If we had known then what we know now about nicotine, there is no way cigarettes would be legal today," said Mr Dillon. "The point is that it would be safer if people did not use a particular drug until we knew everything about it."

Paul Dillon believes it's the responsibility of parents to educate their children about alcohol and drugs. "You can't leave it all up to the schools and the government. You can't blame peer pressure all the time, either. The relationship kids have with their parents has a strong influence when it comes to making choices and taking risks.

"Nine times out of ten, kids who have been educated about drugs will make the right choice," he said. "If they make the wrong choice, hopefully they'll know what to do if things go wrong."

SPEED

Speed (also "go-ee" and "whizz") is the common name for amphetamines. These usually come in the form of white or yellow powder, which is manufactured illegally. Speed can be swallowed, inhaled or injected.

Because there are no controls over how speed is made it is often mixed with other substances which can be harmful.

Amphetamines are stimulants which directly affect the central nervous system by speeding up the way certain chemicals work in the brain. Developed in the United States in the 1920s, amphetamines were once used by doctors to treat depression, obesity and some other conditions. They are now used only rarely for medical problems.

In the 1995 National Drug Strategy household survey, 3 per cent of teenagers said they had tried amphetamines and 2 per cent had used them within the previous twelve months. Despite the fact that research shows speed to be a particularly nasty drug once it takes a hold on users, illegal use seems to be increasing. While some people take speed to "get high", others take it to stay awake, and to drive themselves further during work, study or sport.

Effects vary but amphetamines generally reduce appetite, increase breathing and pulse rate, increase blood pressure, increase alertness and induce a feeling of self-confidence and energy; they cause insomnia, enlarged pupils, hyperactivity, anxiety, irritability, paranoia and panic attacks. Higher doses cause sweating and headaches, restlessness, shaking and dizziness, and a very rapid or irregular heartbeat, as well as hostility and aggression.

As with the use of most drugs over a prolonged period, the long-term use of speed can lead to malnutrition, unprovoked violence, emotional disturbance and vulnerability to infection. Deaths have occurred as a result of overdoses of amphetamines. People can become dependent on speed and need increasing doses to maintain its effects on them.

Some people take other drugs, such as tranquillisers, alcohol or heroin, to cope with the undesirable effects of taking speed. This leads to the roller-coaster ride which we read about in movie magazines – where drugs are needed to get going at the start of the day and to turn off at night.

Note: Caffeine – found in coffee, tea, cola and cocoa – and cocaine, an illegal drug, which comes in the form of white powder, are stimulants which act similarly to amphetamines; they affect the central nervous system by speeding up certain chemicals in the brain. Cocaine is not usually part of the teenage scene. Caffeine is.

LSD

Hallucinogens are the psychedelic drugs which became well known in the sixties when no pop stars worth their weight in flowers and beads were game to admit they hadn't taken a trip into unreality.

Hallucinogens affect all the senses and, as the name suggests, cause hallucinations; they make people see or hear things which don't exist and can also distort thinking, time and emotion.

Some plants and seeds contain hallucinogenic properties, but the best known chemically produced hallucinogen is LSD (lysergic acid diethylamide), also known as acid. A similar chemical to LSD is psilocybin, which is found in certain mushrooms, also called "magic mushrooms", and is usually sold as dried mushrooms or in mushroom preparations.

Ecstasy and cannabis can also produce hallucinations.

The 1995 National Drug Strategy household survey found that 6 per cent of children aged fourteen to nineteen had ever tried LSD and 5 per cent had used it in the last year.

People who do take LSD don't use it in the excessive amounts that pickled the brains of sixties stars; they are more likely to see one spider on their skin than a million huge hairy ones blanketing their bodies. But like all drugs, it is unpredictable – mental disturbances can result from regular use but a single trip can give an unlucky person panic attacks for up to two years.

When using LSD or "tripping", the intensity of bright colours, and the exaggerated and distorted sights, sounds and feelings can cause a sensation of floating or being pulled down. It also creates swings in emotion and mood, strong anxiety, fear and lack of control. A "bad trip", most common among first-time users of LSD, is when only negative and frightening feelings occur during the drug experience, sometimes resulting in panic or in the person "going crazy". This can lead to injury and even suicide. Usually, but not always, the negative feelings recede as the drug wears off.

However, the most disturbing long-term effect of LSD is the "flashback". Flashbacks can occur days, weeks or even years after the drug is taken and usually involve some kind of hallucination.

The physical symptoms of taking LSD can include numbness, muscle weakness, twitching, dilated pupils, shakiness, poor co-ordination, nausea, vomiting, sweating, chills, shivering, rapid deep breathing and increased heartbeat and blood pressure. Because LSD puts stress on the body, gut problems such as constipation, stomach cramps and diarrhoea are also a fairly common side effect – a far cry from the floating fantasy users are after.

Paul Dillon warned parents that the most dangerous thing about LSD is that a "trip", which looks like a small square of cardboard, can be purchased for twenty dollars and divided among friends. At that price it's cheaper than a packet of cigarettes, and can have a potentially lethal effect on children.

HEROIN

Heroin ("smack") is a "hard" drug even by today's standards and is rarely used by teenagers. Usually injected, it slows down the body and the mind. It is extremely addictive and creates in its victims an insatiable need for more. It is closely linked with aggressive behaviour and criminal activity. Reports suggest that heroin use is increasing in Australia, which means that teenagers may not remain strangers to it for long.

Thousands of teenagers, rich, poor and in-between, from plummy private school students to disgruntled delinquents in disadvantaged areas, from traditional as well as single-parent families, from the country, the city and suburbs, will never try illegal drugs.

A vast majority of those who do won't take the risk more than once in their teenage lifetime.

Most of these young people *will* try alcohol. Most of these young people will never believe drink is a dangerous drug.

The teenagers who come out on top will be the girls and boys who enjoy happy personal relationships, particularly with their families, and who receive and understand the information they are given concerning drug and alcohol abuse.

These are the cool kids whose names will never become statistics on the D-files.

WHAT TO DO WHEN A DRUG GOES WRONG

- HELP is needed when you, or someone you know, becomes ill after taking an illegal drug.
- URGENT treatment is needed if you vomit or feel frightened, uncomfortable or out of control.
- CALL an ambulance.
- GO to a hospital or medical centre.
- TELL medical staff what drug was taken, how much and when.
- LEGAL action is not the concern of the medical staff.
- SAVING LIVES is their top priority.
- Make it your top priority. LEARN from this experience and STOP doing drugs. There are a million better ways to have a good time.

15

JUST FOR KIDS

It was all very well to say "Drink me", but the wise little Alice was not going to do *that* in a hurry. "No, I'll look first," she said, "and see whether it's marked 'poison' or not" . . . she had never forgotten that, if you drink much from a bottle marked "poison", it is almost certain to disagree with you, sooner or later.

(*Alice in Wonderland*, Lewis Carroll)

Okay, kids. This chapter is just for you. Toast a muffin, pour a Coke, grab a bag of chips, chomp an apple (if it won't snap your braces) and then curl up with this and have a read.

Please.

If you're under eighteen and you are thinking about drugs and drug-taking, there's one simple question you could ask. WHY?

No, not why kids do drugs. We've been there and done that.

Instead ask why not? WHY should you NOT take them? WHY are drugs against the law? Or more accurately, WHY is the law against drugs – and especially, against kids taking drugs?

They make you feel woozily wonderful. Some give you heaps of temporary energy. Others make you see ordinary things in a strange and special way. Lots of people are taking them without any obvious short-term ill effects. You're just curious and you probably won't do it very much anyway. You know for sure that *you'll* never get addicted. So WHY should it be against the law to put one or two, or maybe three or four, drugs into your bodies? WHY?

Come on, kids. You've been brought up to question, to argue, to challenge, to demand your rights. You're allowed to answer back when you think your parents are not making sense, to interrupt your teachers, to accuse adults of damaging the earth you'll inherit, to confront the older generation with their neglect of the environment, to have opinions, to think for yourselves.

It's illegal to sell cigarettes or alcohol to children under the age of eighteen. WHY?

It's illegal for people of any age to take certain drugs – such as marijuana, speed, LSD, ecstasy, cocaine, heroin. WHY?

You know WHY you're interested in taking them. It's because you're not supposed to. But WHY are you not supposed to? WHY are drugs forbidden?

WHY have the governments of countries all over the world gone to the trouble of making drugs illegal? WHY do they sign international treaties to ensure that drugs stay illegal? WHY?

Is it because adults want to have all the fun? Is it because they can't stand to see kids enjoying themselves?

Is it to give the police something to do, because other crimes are so few and far between? Is it because governments are dying to spend millions of dollars chasing illegal drug importers and manufacturers so they can put them in gaol and spend even more millions of dollars supporting them in a lifestyle to which they are not accustomed? (Luckily for them, not for long – they'll be out again really soon and living much more comfortably than you and me.)

Drugs are a big headache for the people who make and administer the laws that control our society. They are an even bigger headache for parents whose children take or might take them.

Of course, as far as some kids are concerned, drugs are fun, exciting, different. The wheeling and dealing, the meetings, the secret codes, the thrill of getting away with it – that's part of the pleasure, part of the play. Half the time those kids are taking them *because* they are illegal. So why, why, WHY do governments and parents bother to try to control them – and you – at all?

Why doesn't authority just shrug its tailored shoulders and say: Go for it? WHY?

The answer is that these drugs contain varying amounts of poison.

Poison is an old-fashioned word but most of you know what it means. Snakes are scarier if they are poisonous – it means they can kill you. The most hideous spiders are the poisonous ones. They can kill you too, or paralyse you or make you ill. Anything with poison in it can kill you or disable you or make you ill.

Poison can be defined as any substance that impairs health or destroys life when swallowed, inhaled or absorbed by the body in relatively small amounts. Another word that means poisonous is "toxic".

One of the reasons poisoning is still such a frightening prospect for most people is that there are relatively few effective medicines or antidotes capable of curing anyone who has been poisoned. Treatment is usually limited to the removal of the toxic material from the body as quickly as possible after it is taken and before it is absorbed.

People who don't want to risk getting sick or dying avoid taking poison. It's why cleaning fluid and detergent and paint and every other manufactured chemical mixture not meant for human consumption is marked POISON.

Illicit drugs are potentially poisonous but there's one big difference. They don't have a tag.

They are not marked "poison" because the last thing the people selling them want you to know is that they contain poison, possibly in dangerous amounts, or that they may be harmful.

Most adolescents are too smart to knowingly pour something marked POISON down their throats.

Younger kids do, of course. As they're smaller, toxic chemicals can kill them quite quickly. Adolescents are almost fully grown. The damage poison can do to them is not always obvious until later. Maybe much later. It doesn't mean the damage isn't being done.

Poison does bad things to the human body. Poison makes your system react in a way it isn't designed to. Poison makes you sick. Poison can kill. If you are as unlucky as Anna Wood, it can kill you dead.

If you are more fortunate, it will only kill parts of you – those areas of your brain which make you so uniquely *you*. Drugs will kill your initiative, your energy, your ideas, your imagination, your hopes, your ambitions, your dreams.

As Alice knew when she arrived in Wonderland, poison will almost certainly disagree with you, sooner or later.

All drugs are not the same. But all drugs, both legal and illegal, both medical and "recreational", have the potential to do harm.

"Recreational" means "for enjoyment". Remember, every drug addict took their first drug for enjoyment. Anna Wood took ecstasy for enjoyment. A lot of kids take their first drug – their first swig, or puff, or tablet – just for fun, or simply out of curiosity. Most are intelligent enough not to do it again. For those who do, the fun and the interest don't last; these kids end up doing drugs just for the drug's sake. They are hooked.

Whenever a new pharmaceutical drug is developed it has to be tested for years before it is allowed to be sold for human consumption. Even so, some get through. Thalidomide is a classic example – a drug that was meant to help pregnant women but was found to cause terrible deformities in their babies.

Over the years, the development of new drugs has become more and more rigidly controlled to prevent such tragedies. By the time a pharmaceutical drug becomes available for use in medical treatment, scientists and doctors know everything about it. They know precise measurements of every chemical it contains. They know the short and long-term effects it will have on human beings. These drugs cannot be prescribed by doctors or sold by chemists except to help sick people. Sometimes even these medicines have unpleasant side effects.

No chemicals should be put into your body unless they are prescribed for you because you are ill.

Lead was used in the manufacture of many household items, including paint and petrol, before its toxic effects were discovered. Now that scientists have found that lead can cause brain damage and other illnesses because of its poisonous content, every effort is being made to remove lead from our environment.

Many chemicals, including bromides, mercury, DDT, lead and asbestos, are no longer used in the manufacture of different products, because they were found to be very injurious to people's health. These substances are now controlled by strict laws.

There are no such controls on the way illegal drugs are produced. As a result, it is impossible to know for sure what's in them. A great deal is known about the short-term effects of illegal drugs and the dangers of these, but very little research has been done on their long-term effects on people.

What *is* known is that they contain chemicals which have a toxic or poisonous effect on the body and that is why their use is regulated or banned by the government.

Adults who take such drugs are taking an enormous risk. It's a risk nobody wants children taking.

Governments come and go; whatever their politics may be, these days they receive limited respect and a great deal of criticism. But one thing all democratic governments aim to do is to protect children. No government will pass any laws which leave children vulnerable to harm.

That's why, in Australia, children are not allowed to drink alcohol. Large amounts of alcohol can poison them. Boys – and girls – who binge drink are consuming enough grog to kill them or do their bodies permanent harm.

It's also why children are not allowed to smoke. Tobacco will poison them. It's why children are not allowed to take illicit drugs. They will poison them.

Of course, adults aren't allowed to take illicit drugs either. They believe the decision should be up to them. Unfortunately, governments spend millions of dollars every year in the areas of health and social services, trying to repair the damage that adults have done to themselves and their families by making decisions which led to their abuse of drugs. Enormous amounts of the money working people pay in taxes has to be allocated to the needs of the victims of drug abuse, the ill, the dying, the depressed, the divorced, the despairing – the smokers, the drinkers, and the addicts.

Adults *are* allowed to smoke, although now that they know about the poison in tobacco, most civilised governments are beavering away to make it as hard as possible for their citizens to keep doing it. Many adults would like to give up smoking but they can't stop because they are addicted to tobacco. Like people who are hooked on illegal drugs, no cigarette smoker ever intended to become addicted. It just happened. There's no reason for you kids to make the same mistake.

Adults *are* allowed to drink alcohol because it's assumed that they are sensible and mature enough to know how to drink in moderation.

What a calm and rational community we would have if that was true of everybody over the age of eighteen!

Alcohol and cigarettes have been around for centuries, although that doesn't make them any less harmful. Medical research has now given you the truth about what they do to your bodies. Past generations of teenagers didn't know how dangerous cigarettes and alcohol were. You kids have no such excuse.

Adults often let down the side by not behaving in an adult fashion.

One of the worst things adults have done in the past thirty-five years in particular, is to allow the development of the idea that taking drugs is a natural part of life.

It's not.

There is nothing natural about polluting your body with poison.

Since the sixties, when marijuana first became very popular in Western countries, certain sections of society have spread the mistaken belief that adolescents have always used so-called "soft" drugs (that is, drugs which are likely to kill or damage fewer rather than many people) in order to expand their view of life.

They haven't.

Drugs other than alcohol and cigarettes have never been used by the general population. In previous civilisations, even the quite sophisticated ones, witchdoctors and priests dabbled in dangerous mind-altering chemicals to reach a mystic state. In modern times, some artists, musicians and creative people have dabbled in drugs for similar reasons, often with tragic results. But for ordinary people, for hundreds of years, drugs (with the exception of wine) have never been a natural part of life.

Since when has taking poison been common?

Since when has altering your brain chemistry with toxic substances been a normal thing to do?

Kids are being conditioned to believe that experimenting with drugs is normal; that way the people selling drugs create a demand for their product.

The people who push drugs in our society are very clever. They know if you say anything often enough, people start to believe it. With enough repetition, people get used to anything.

Two hundred years ago, if you used the word "damn" in front of a lady, she was in danger of fainting.

Forty years ago if you said "shit" in public you could get arrested.

Now there's the F word. Once it was shocking. Now people say fuck so often, on the movies, on the television, on the street, in the parks and yards of the suburbs, that soon it won't be shocking any more. Those who like to shock will have to think of a new word to attract attention.

Thirty years ago teenagers puffed a quick ciggy in the sand dunes and thought they were being brave.

If inhaling poison is brave, they were.

A certain percentage of today's teenagers puff ciggies, inhale cannabis, swallow amphetamines, swig beer, vodka and rum, and gulp the occasional E. They are taking their poison in greater amounts and needing more and more of it to achieve the required brain change.

Is that brave?

What is particularly disgusting is that during the last ten or twenty years, you kids haven't been told the truth. A lot of wrong information has been handed out to pharmacists and doctors, too, but none of it compares with the massive number of lies which have been fed to children about illegal drugs.

Kids today are not like the adolescents of thirty and forty years ago. You kids want answers. You deserve to be told the truth.

Simply telling you not to take drugs isn't good enough. You should be given all the information available about what drugs will do to you. You should be told WHY using these chemicals is against the law.

A writer recently suggested, in a popular magazine, that kids needed to take poisonous drugs to "escape the pain of being human".

Sadly, some of you may be abused, poverty-stricken or desperately ill. You are the exceptions to the rule that most Australian children are born full of joy and good health. Is it so strange that your parents are horrified when some of you reach your teens and try to have fun by swallowing, sniffing, inhaling or drinking poison?

Escaping the pain? Anna Wood and her friends weren't trying to escape from pain. They were looking for excitement – but by taking poison they found more pain than they had ever thought possible.

In the same article it was suggested that rave parties are fabulous as long as there are trained medical people and para-medics standing by.

Well, guys, have you seriously reached the stage where you and your friends can't have a good party – a great night of fun, music, dancing, talking – without lining up some paramedics?

"Okay Mum, Dad, it's okay for you to go out now. We've got four crates of Coke, eight bags of burger buns and Steve's dad is letting him have heaps of sausages from his shop; we've asked everyone to bring their favourite CDs and Lisa's going to book the paramedics."

Paramedics?

People who are spreading the word that it's natural to take drugs, that fun is only possible with the assistance of drugs – whether those drugs are alcohol, tobacco or illicit drugs like ecstasy, speed and LSD – are not only advocating the poisoning of your minds and bodies. They are poisoning your spirit.

The real meaning of the word ecstasy is joy. Illegal drugs and the people who sell and promote them are stealing away the joy you all deserve, the joy that is your birthright – the joy of being human.

Ask WHY.

"GOD'S LENT CHILD"
(Author unknown)

I'll lend you for a little time
A child of mine, God said.
For you to love her while she lives
and mourn for when she's dead.
It may be six or seven years,
Or twenty-two or three,
but will you, till I call her back,
Take care of her for me?
She'll bring her charms to gladden you
And shall her stay be brief,
You'll have her lovely memories
As solace for your grief.
I cannot promise she will stay
Since all from earth return
But there are lessons taught down there
I want this child to learn.
I've looked the wide world over

In my search for teachers true
And from the throngs that crowd life's lane
I have selected you.
Now will you give her all your love
Nor think the labour vain
Nor hate me when I come to call
To take her back again.
I fancied that I heard them say,
Dear Lord, thy will be done,
For all the joy thy child shall bring
The risk of grief we'll run.
We'll shelter her with tenderness,
We'll love her while we may,
And for the happiness we've known
Forever grateful stay.
But shall the angels call for her
Much sooner than we've planned,
We'll brave the bitter grief that comes
And try to understand.

PART TWO

······································

WONDERLAND

". . . for it might end, you know . . . in my going out altogether,
like a candle."
(*Alice in Wonderland*, Lewis Carroll)

Above left: *Angela and Anna in Manly, 1992.*
Above right: *Anna with Alice, 1995.*
Below left: *The socialite.*   Below right: *Anna at rest.*

16

SATURDAY NIGHT

Anna was high as the sky on pure, natural excitement as she raced into the house late on Saturday afternoon. She had just done her first eyelash tint at the beauty salon. Her boss, Gayle, had gone home with thicker, lovelier lashes and not a smudge anywhere. At last Anna was a real beautician!

No more boring school and dreary books! No more assignments ever! No more letters apologising to the teachers for not working hard enough. Now she had something worth trying for. She was earning her living just the way she had always wanted to – by making people beautiful! Just two more weeks and she'd be doing it full-time.

George and Alexia had driven her home from work. They had cheered when she told them about the eyelash tint and she had bowed, in the middle of the street, and even the people in the salon had cracked up. Life was so good!

They had come to pick her up so they could talk her into going with them to the rave party tonight. A real rave in a city club! Did she dare?

Last night, when they were all together around at Mick's,* it seemed like a very exciting idea. George had suggested it. George was a real raver, he had been to so many. Alexia thought it was a terrific idea, of course. It would be *so* wicked.

They were dying to know if she would be allowed out so she could go with them. It would be *so* exciting if she could. But it wasn't going to be easy. She'd have to be careful about getting away. It would be necessary to play it cool with Dad. Please please please, she thought, let him say yes.

An hour later, about 6.30 p.m., Angela Wood arrived home from work. It had been another long day at the office. For months Angela had been feeling that she spent more time at work than at home. Thank heavens tomorrow was Sunday.

The Wood family lived in a modern, two-storey house in a small and quiet cul-de-sac, pleasantly close to the coast. Commuters loaded up the nearby Forest Way with droning cars every peak hour, but tucked away on a neat suburban chessboard, the Wood's home seemed a long way from the roar of the traffic and the smell of the fumes.

The house was full of happy noise and cooking aromas. In the big kitchen, with its crammed pantry and bench tops cluttered with notes and newspapers, flowers, baskets of fruit and ripening avocados, Tony Wood was preparing the evening meal.

"There's going to be seven of us tonight, love," he said, and she could tell he was pleased and excited. His entire family would be sitting down together for one of his spectacular dinners.

Tony had been away so much lately, going wherever the company sent him, in order to get some money into the bank after the financial blow their failed business had dealt them. Tonight, for a little while, they were all together again. This would be a very special evening.

Glenda, Tony's daughter from his first marriage, and her little girl, Kristina, aged four, had come over for tea. Julie, their exchange student from Quebec, would be eating with them too. Alice and Anna were both at home. Angela was delighted. Tony would be sharing a meal with all the women he loved most in his life. Better still – he was cooking it!

"Tony, Glenda and I were trying to talk in the kitchen and there was so much noise coming from the living room that we had to shout at them to quieten down," said Angela. "Anna and little Kristina were playing Twister and they were giggling hysterically, laughing and thumping about. We couldn't hear ourselves think.

"Then Anna poked her head into the kitchen to see what we were yelling about. I asked her if she was going out after dinner. After all, it was Saturday night."

"No," said Anna, looking reasonably unconcerned. "Dad says I can't."

"Were you planning anything?" asked Angela.

"Oh, we were just going over to Chloe's," said Anna casually. "We were going to watch a few videos with George and Alexia."

Tony turned around and looked quizzically at his daughter. "Oh, all right," he sighed. "You can go. You get around me, don't you?"

Angela was glad. "It's that guilt thing you have when you're a mother of teenagers. Fancy keeping your fifteen-year-old daughter in on a Saturday night just because you say so! All she wanted to do was go and watch videos with friends. She'd done it before. It seemed an acceptable Saturday night activity. Both Anna and Alice occasionally went out with friends and then brought them back here to stay for the night. Or they would sleep at their friends' houses. Only on Saturdays, of course. It was taboo on school nights.

"I feel guilty that I didn't check that she was where she said she would be. But on the other Saturday nights it had all been fine – I picked her up the next morning, she was always there and we never had a problem.

"Tony told me she had been on the phone for ages when she got home from work. I suppose she and her friends were making plans. But she had never given us any reason not to trust her."

"I changed my mind because she was such a good kid," said Tony. "She was playing around on the floor with Kristina. She hadn't even argued with me about going out. If she had, I would probably have dug my heels in. But she was happy. She knew if I said no I meant it and that was that."

Alexia was thrilled that Anna was allowed out after all.

"On Friday night we had all been together at Mick's house, and George had told us about the rave party in the city. We discussed whether we should go. Anna thought she might be able to come with us but she wasn't sure.

"George and I went to see her at the place where she worked on Saturday afternoon. She was busy so she said to come back when she finished work. We gave her a lift home but she still didn't know if she could get away.

"I rang her after she had been home for a while and she said she couldn't go with us.

"We were so disappointed that we would have to go without her. Then she rang me back and said she could go after all. I phoned George and said: 'Anna's coming now, Anna's coming now,' and George said: 'That's good,' and we went to Pete's house and woke him up – 'Come on, come on, we're going to a rave and Anna's coming, Anna's coming.'"

Tony cooked filet mignon for the family. It was a lovely meal. There was talk and laughter. Alice, who had been studying all day for her final school examination, welcomed the break. Kristina and Anna finished off with strawberries and ice-cream.

When the meal was over, Anna jumped up and went upstairs to get her backpack and her overnight clothes. She was wearing loose jeans, a short white top and a navy jumper; she had released her smooth straight hair from its ponytail.

She came back and hugged her father. "Thanks for letting me go, Pop," she said.

"She hugged us all," said Julie. "It was usual for her to kiss her parents but she hugged each of us before she left. She was very excited."

Alice remembers George coming into the room and her father speaking to him as he and Anna left together. "You're responsible for Anna this evening," Tony said. "Sure," said George, "don't worry, everything's going to be fine."

George doesn't remember speaking to Tony at all.

George and Anna went out the front door. "We didn't know she was being picked up in a car outside," said Angela. "Chloe only lives in the next street, so we thought they were walking. We didn't know she was going to any sort of party.

"We didn't know at that moment when she left us, that it was the last time she would really be our Anna."

When Anna slid into the back seat of George's green mini, beside Pete, the sixth member of the Baboona clan, she was very excited, but she had a bit of business to take care of first. "George," she said. "We've decided I'm staying at your place tonight, okay? Watching videos."

George and Alexia were in the front seat. "Yeah, okay," he said, starting the motor.

It was a clear night. The earlier rain had dragged itself to a sulky stop. George drove them to North Head, a cliff-top lookout with a spectacular view of ocean. They liked to park there and talk.

"We discussed going to Apache, the rave party, and whether it was worth it because we didn't know for sure whether we would get in," said Alexia.

Nobody remembers who first brought up the subject of taking ecstasy. They had talked about that, too, the previous night; a rave would not be a real rave without it. Anna had been wary; now it seemed like a much better idea. "We didn't talk about anything else, apart from going to the rave and taking ecstasy," said Alexia. "I mean, what else would there be to talk about?"

The girls decided to buy one tablet and take half each, as they had done at a local dance party in August. That had been a good night. The biggest problem had been finding a place to wait until it was late enough on the Sunday morning to go home. They had mooched around a local park.

"George and Pete weren't as excited as us," said Alexia. "Then they had this idea of maybe finding a motel room somewhere in the city so that if we couldn't get into the rave, we could go there. We could still buy an E and take it there."

This was a new and exciting idea that the unsophisticated fifteen-year-olds had never entertained before. Staying overnight in the city, having a room where the four of them could talk for hours, maybe have a little picnic, watch some telly – if the rave party proved to be impossible, this would be better than doing nothing. A lot better! Not surprisingly, the older boys thought so too.

"We drove into the city," said George, "and we stopped at two or three motels but they all had no vacancy signs. Everything was booked up. So in the end we went to Ultimo, to the club where Apache, the dance party, was on."

The club is in George Street, in the heart of Broadway, just outside the central business district of the city. A red neon sign is the only feature that distinguishes it from a line of faceless buildings which carry the grime from years of passing traffic. Cars drone by in a monotonous stream.

On a quiet night the club looks like a corner pub. That Saturday, because there was a rave on, crowds of people, most of them in their twenties or younger, were crowded on the footpath outside, talking, laughing, wheeling and dealing in the dark.

Anna and her friends arrived well after midnight. George parked the car down a side street. By this time they were very wound up about the prospect of buying an ecstasy tablet and getting "high".

"I don't know why Anna decided to do it that night," said George. "We knew it would be available if we wanted it. But I mean, she hadn't wanted to take it before, sort of thing."

"You don't have to plan to get ecstasy. You know if it's a rave party, people will be there selling it. It's part of the scene."

They walked down to the club. Pete, who was nineteen and therefore not under age, bought a ticket and went inside. George and the girls looked around for somebody who would be able to provide them with some ecstasy.

They didn't have to look far. A Year Twelve student from their school who had been a source of drugs for the past two years was standing on the footpath, waiting for business.

"We all knew her and we knew she'd know where we could get some E," said Alexia. "So we went up to her and asked and she said she had some. She had the tablets with her, in a black bag."

The girl accompanied the three of them back to George's car. She climbed into the back seat with George and handed over his tablet. George said she charged him the standard price of sixty dollars.

George then got out of the car and Alexia and Anna climbed into the back seat and bought an ecstasy tablet, paying thirty dollars each. According to Alexia, the tablets were in small plastic bags.

All four then walked back to the club but when they arrived Alexia had second thoughts. "We were hanging around outside the club and we were both saying we would have liked a whole one. We thought half a one might not work as well. So I went back up to the girl, just outside the club, and said: 'D'you reckon you could let us have another one on tick? Like, we'll pay you back another day, when we get the money?' She said: 'That's fine, not a problem.' We went around the corner and she put one in my hand. It wasn't in a plastic bag like the others. Then we came back and waited outside with everyone else. They were mostly kids and they were all just chatting. There were quite a few people there we knew."

Nobody thought it was unusual that two fifteen-year-old girls had joined the crowd. In their jeans and cotton tops, Anna and Alexia looked just like everybody else. Nobody too old goes to raves, Alexia explained, and you don't get dressed up. Nobody notices what anyone is wearing.

When they saw Chloe and her friend Suzie* arrive, they were surprised, pleased and not a little relieved. Anna was concerned that Chloe had not been included in the plans for the evening – and now, here she was! All the Baboonas, with the exception of Kathie, were together for a great time!

Poor Kath. She always had heaps of money but she still had her problems. Sometimes her mother was just too smart. Parents could be such a pain!

Chloe and Suzie had been to Manly for the evening and had then made their way into the city. Finding little to do, they decided to walk down Broadway to see if there was any chance of getting into the rave at the club. They had no tickets and little money, but they knew there was always a good chance of sneaking past the bouncers at events like these.

A thin, dark man was making his way through the crowds outside the club, offering his wares to the would-be ravers. Chloe and Suzie bought a "trip" of LSD from him, paying nineteen dollars fifty for it – fifty cents short of the right price because that was all Suzie had. Chloe had no money at all.

The "trip", on a small piece of what looked like blotting paper, and only about a centimetre square, had to be divided between both girls. They split it, swallowed it and waited for it to take them somewhere. Disappointingly, they both remained exactly where they were.

"We sat outside on the edge of the gutter for about half an hour and then we saw the others," said Chloe. "Anna and Alexia came and gave us both a big hug. They said they'd got their Es. They were pretty excited."

Chloe told them she had taken a trip which hadn't worked. She asked her friends who had sold them their Es and when she heard that one had been provided "on tick" by someone from school, she asked whether more might be available. Anna shook her head.

"We paid for two of them and she gave us one but don't ask her for any more on tick." It was typical of Anna – she thought asking for more credit would have meant stretching the bounds of such a tenuous relationship too far.

Meanwhile, George had bought a ticket and entered the club. He wanted to get some water so they could all wash down their tablets. Ecstasy tablets are difficult to take, he explained, and taste "vile".

George met a friend inside and they started talking. Half an hour slipped by.

Anna and Alexia grew tired of waiting for George. The crowds of people surged around them, laughing and greeting each other with shouts and hugs. They could hear the music pounding inside. The two girls grew impatient. They wanted to be part of it. They wanted something to happen to them.

"We decided not to wait for George any longer," said Alexia. "I asked someone if we could borrow their bottle of water and we went around the corner. Anna said: 'This is so exciting.' We took our ecstasy tablets and we washed them down with the water."

When Chloe saw Anna and Alexia return to the club entrance, about fifteen minutes later, she said Anna was excited but slightly anxious. There seemed to be some question as to whether it had been wise to take a full E each, rather than half an E then and the other half later.

George came out of the club shortly afterwards to be greeted with the news that his protégées had taken their Es without his assistance.

"I thought we were all going to take them together," said George later. "I had brought water for them. Anyway, I went around the corner and had mine. I only had half. They wanted me to have a full one, they were trying to make me. I said: 'No way!' I have taken ecstasy about fifteen times. I was much more experienced in it than they were."

George took the two girls for a walk up to a park, a few blocks away, so they could all go to the toilet. They returned to the club and George reasserted his senior status by taking Alexia firmly by the arm and simply marching her through the doors, past the bouncers, past the woman on the desk, cool as you like.

"I left her by the poker machines and told her to wait," said George. "Then I went back, took Anna by the hand and walked her inside as well. None of the security people who were there to check tickets and stamps stopped us. It was easy."

The beat filled their heads as soon as they entered the club. They were in a dimly lit room full of poker machines, but the pulse of the music from the dance floor beyond reverberated around them. Techno music relies heavily on a repetitive thudding beat. It is raucous, continuous, monotonous and loud. Some numbers have limited lyrics and these, too, are repeated over and over and over, with no discernible change in key.

"Your house is my house," chanted an unknown vocalist.

"YourhouseismyhouseYourhouseismyhouseYourhouseis myhouse . . ."

The girls found themselves in the club lounge, with interior decoration in basic plastic; there were tables and chairs and a bar. Beyond that, in a larger room, coloured lances of laser light chased each other across the dance floor. Illuminated by green, red and purple strobes, crowds of people writhed and jerked to the grating techno beat.

You don't dress up for raves. The boys wore T-shirts and baggy pants or jeans; many wore caps and sunglasses. The girls were in T-shirts or tight little tank tops with jeans and the occasional skirt. Their hair was limp and sleek with sweat, their faces shone. People passed bottled water from hand to hand and swigged it thirstily.

If it hadn't been for the dark and the spectacular lighting, they could all have been at the beach.

None of them was very old.

Like high priests on a pagan altar, the disc jockeys sat beneath a red and green symbol on a raised stage. The dancers massed in front of them, gazing up, resembling worshippers as

151

they jerked, gestured and ground their hips on the crowded dance floor; there wasn't much room to move but it didn't matter. This sort of dancing required no fancy foot movement, there were no steps to learn.

A huge banner had been hung from the stage by some of the dancers. It bore a black and lime green "e" on a purple background. Because it was a small "e" rather than a capital, the letter appeared to be grinning knowingly at the panting crowd. Perhaps, after all, it was "e" and not the music that the thirsty ravers had come to worship.

Overhead a green "A" for Apache hung from the ceiling, with nets of balloons, proclaiming the spirit of the rave. Another sign announced that November '95 was the beginning of a New World.

"Welcome to the present," announced a dancing girl, appearing on the stage between songs. "Prepare for peace, love and freedom." She was imprisoned in a cage created from strips of white light.

"The dance is begun," said the girl, while the audience hooted impatiently. "The past is over. Apache is the future."

It wasn't too different from the Age of Aquarius which heralded the New World thirty years ago – except that the boys now had short or shaven hair and the songs, or chants were singularly lacking in originality: "Fuckthewholeparty . . . fuckthewholepartyfuckthewholeparty . . ."

Anna and Alexia looked at each other, eyes round with wonder at their own wickedness in being there. Yes! They were *in*!

George led them past the bar and they sat down at a table with some people they knew. They all had a drink of water. But the girls' feet were twitching. It was probably about two o'clock in the first pounding hours of Sunday morning and they felt that enough time had been wasted. Alexia, short, plump and brimming with excitement, headed towards the dancing. George asked Anna if she wanted to dance.

"She was talking softly and her voice had a different tone to it," said George. "She was really happy and smiley – like other people I had seen under the effects of ecstasy."

Anna, tall, slender, overflowing with exhilaration, rose from her seat and walked with the slight, clean-cut Greek boy towards the dance floor.

The beat caught them up and they started to dance.

17

DAWN

There were a lot of people at Apache who knew Anna. She called greetings, laughed, drank water and danced with some of them. For a long time she danced beside George at the front of the dance floor.

Already Anna's natural joy and energy were rising to an abnormal and frenzied level. The chemical was working on her brain, making her body do strange things and altering her state of mind to a degree most children and many adults could not even begin to imagine.

No longer was she the Anna Wood her family and friends had known. A being invaded by MDMA, she was now a girl pulsing with "ecstasy", jerking and swaying to Apache's lethal beat.

From time to time George and Anna went to the toilets to get water. Neither of them drank any alcohol. Now and then they rested.

"It was really hot and Anna asked if we could sit down for a while," said George. "We went and sat on some stairs away from the dance floor, where it wasn't so loud or hot.

"We stayed there for about half an hour and talked. Anna's water bottle was empty so she went into the toilet to fill it up. She was still acting as if she was under the influence of the ecstasy."

They began dancing again and after a while George told Anna he was going outside to see whether Chloe, the neglected Baboona, was still there.

Anna danced on, alone yet surrounded by a sea of people.

"George took the others in," said Chloe. "I couldn't go in as I didn't have any money or tickets or anything. Well, neither did they, but he sneaked them past the people on the door. He came out a bit later and tried to sneak me in too, but the lady at the desk wanted to see my stamp and because I didn't have one, I had to go back outside.

"My friend Suzie gave up and went home but I stayed there and started talking to a friend of mine, a boy called Jeff.* George came out again and talked to us both. Then he went back inside."

Anna was still dancing when George returned without Chloe. They danced together for a while, but Anna wanted to return to the toilets for more water. George continued dancing by himself for nearly an hour. "You don't have to dance with other people," he said. "The dance is the thing you're there for. The dance and the drug."

Alexia, too, spent the night dancing. "I was going crazy on the dance floor. I danced and danced. I was in my own world. I remember seeing Anna in front of me, smiling and dancing. I could see it was really affecting her. I asked her heaps of times if she was all right and she said: 'Yeah, yeah, I'm terrific! I'm having the best night of my life.'"

"I'm having the best night of my life," repeated Anna to her friends. "I'm having the best night of my life. The best night of my life. The best night of my life." It was like a mantra, dictated by the foreign substance which had invaded and claimed her as its own.

Alexia thinks it was about 5 a.m. when she noticed Anna sitting on a boy's lap at the edge of the dance floor.

"I went up to talk to her and I could see from her face that she was really drugged out. Her face was everywhere, her eyes were rolling around in her head, she was sweating. Her jaw was wobbling. She was clenching and unclenching her fists. Her facial movements kept changing.

"All this was happening to me as well, of course. It's what happens to you on E. I went to get a glass of water and when I came back, she'd gone."

At about 4 a.m. Chloe finally managed to get through the single brown door of the club without being stopped. Her friend Jeff followed. The music met them with a bellow of welcome and they danced for a short time, until Jeff gave Chloe some money so she could play the poker machines.

"After about an hour," said Chloe, "I saw Anna sitting at a table with a boy, another friend of ours, and I went over to talk to them. I could see she'd had her E. She was the full hap. I asked her how she was. She said she was having the best night of her life. Then she grinned and said: 'I think I'm going to throw up.'"

Anna's face was pale and waxy. She vomited, splashing the boy she was with and the other people beside them. Horrified, she leapt up and ran towards the toilets.

"I ran in after her," said Chloe. "I got there just as she collapsed. I caught her and sat her down on the floor, so she could heave into the toilet bowl. I started to scream. There was such a big mess and she was throwing up heaps."

"I'm sorry, I'm sorry," gasped Anna as she retched. "I'm feeling so awful. I hate this feeling. I want it to go away."

George was out getting some chewing gum from his car; he returned just in time to see Anna start running towards the toilet. She was vomiting as she ran. Chloe went after her.

"I went to get Alexia so we could find out what was happening," said George.

"I asked this guy where she was," said Alexia, "and he said she had just thrown up on him.

"Of course my first instinct was to be with her. George was outside the toilets so I told him to come in too. I could hear her. I could hear her calling me."

They found Anna sitting on the end toilet with the door half open. She was very pale.

"I'm so sorry," Anna was saying piteously. "I'm spoiling your night. I'm sorry. I feel so terrible." Then she vomited again and again.

George took off his T-shirt and they soaked it in water and pressed it against Anna's face.

"I was crying out for somebody to help us," said Alexia. "Then this girl came and said she was a nurse, so I asked her what we should do.

"She'll be fine," said the nurse. "She's just had a bad E. Give her lots of water, take her home and put her to sleep."

"Where am I?" said Anna angrily. "What are you doing? I want to go home. I want to go home."

"We wet her face," said Chloe. "But she started not remembering things. There were auditions for drama the next day and I reminded her she had to get better to be there, but she didn't know what I was talking about.

"She started apologising again for ruining our night. Then she slipped back into it again and didn't seem to know what was going on."

George went to wait outside the women's toilets. A little later, while Chloe waited helplessly for Anna to recover, Alexia also left the toilets. She asked another boy to help her and Chloe get Anna out into the fresh air.

The boy, who also knew Anna, gave her a drink of water and stroked her hair, before helping her to her feet. The three teenagers then half dragged, half carried Anna through the lounge and the small lobby, which was not much bigger than the average kitchen.

"There was a woman sitting at the desk and the security people were still at the front of the club," said Chloe. "But we sort of dragged Anna past and none of them said anything. We didn't ask them for help."

Outside, a moody dawn had broken. The rain from the day before had cleared.

"Please," muttered Anna, as they lowered her down onto the footpath, "please don't think I'm stupid."

"I told her what was happening," said Alexia. "I was trying to get her back into reality. We sat her down outside and kept giving her water and I gave her a little massage to calm her down.

"She said she was feeling a bit better so we decided to take her home."

George came out and found his friends sitting on the footpath looking far from ecstatic about the way their great night was turning out.

There were still about twenty people outside the club, according to Chloe's estimate. Some of them knew the Baboonas and told police later that they had noticed that Anna wasn't herself. None of these people and none of Anna's friends suggested that a doctor, ambulance, or hospital might be needed. People got sick all the time from ecstasy and other drugs. It was nothing new.

The sixth Baboona, Pete, had spent the night playing the poker machines, chatting to friends and watching the dancing from the mezzanine level at the club. At dawn he returned to George's car but when nobody turned up he went back to the club, only to find the distressed group outside the entrance. When he told them to calm down he enraged Chloe, who pushed him roughly. Angry words were exchanged.

"He was being so arrogant," said Alexia. "We were already upset and worried and his arrogant attitude didn't help." Pete then walked off, leaving the miserable group to sort out its problems without him.

"Chloe's friend Jeff hadn't taken anything," said George. "I asked him if he would drive Anna and Chloe home, because I wasn't sure if I was safe to drive. I'd only taken half an E when we arrived but it was wearing off and I had taken the second half just before Anna got sick."

Chloe and Alexia also claim credit for getting Jeff to drive Anna home. Well – almost home. Chloe decided Anna should be taken to her place, just around the corner from Anna's house. She told George and Alexia she didn't want them to come over until later in the morning. It was too early; she would have too much explaining to do if her mother woke up and found the house full of people.

"Jeff said he was cool so we all started walking around the corner towards his car," said George. "Then Anna said, 'Hang on a minute, I've just got to sit down,' and she sat on the footpath again and it seemed like she was vomiting but nothing was coming out of her mouth.

"We left Anna with Jeff and Chloe while Alexia and I went to my car and got her jumper and her bag. Then I asked Jeff to bring his car around so Anna wouldn't have to walk far, and that's what he did.

"Anna was still talking. She kept saying how sorry she was for spoiling our night."

Alexia ordered somebody to bring a plastic bag in case Anna felt ill again on the way home. "Then we put her in Jeff's car and I gave her a kiss and said I'd be there soon."

As soon as she slumped into the back seat, Anna began retching again. She was still conscious and still talking but she looked pale and ill.

It was a forty-minute drive to Belrose. "On the way, she said she couldn't feel her lips or her legs," said Chloe. "I asked her if she thought we should take her to see a doctor, but she didn't answer. She didn't seem to know who she was or where she was."

When they reached Chloe's house, Jeff helped Anna out of the car while Chloe went ahead and quickly made up one of the twin beds in her room for Anna.

When she ran quietly downstairs and out to the car again, Jeff was looking concerned. He had given drunk and drugged friends a lift before, but there was something really strange about the way Anna was acting.

"Chloe," he said, "Anna doesn't know who I am. She's really scared. She doesn't know what she's doing."

Chloe took Anna's hand and stared into her face. "Anna, sweetheart," she whispered, "it's Chloe. We're going upstairs to my room."

"Who're you?" slurred Anna. "What're you doing?"

Chloe helped her to walk as far as the front door but on the porch Anna collapsed and vomited again. Chloe left her with Jeff and went inside to make some orange juice and sugar. She remembered hearing that this might help.

She was wrong.

"I took the glass outside and put it into Anna's hands and she took a sip. Then she dropped it; the glass just fell out of her hands."

Chloe and Jeff pushed Anna through the front door and up the stairs to Chloe's bedroom. She vomited on the way. They put her into bed and she seemed to fall instantly asleep.

"We left her in bed and tried to clean up the mess on the stairs," said Chloe. "Then we heard this big thump and we went up to see what had happened. She was lying against the door and we couldn't get it open. I could hear her vomiting.

"I finally pushed the door open far enough to get in. She'd thrown up on the floor. I put her back into bed. She wasn't talking any more, just retching and throwing up and rolling around on the bed. I tried to look after her but I didn't know what else to do.

"My dad came out of his room and saw Jeff downstairs and told him it was too early for him to be there and to go home. Then Dad went back to bed. He didn't know Anna was in my room.

"Jeff went home then and I rang George on his mobile and asked him and Alex to come over."

After Anna was taken off in Jeff's car, George and Alexia had returned briefly to the club. Not long afterwards they left and began driving home. The effects of their own drugs were wearing off, leaving them exhausted and seedy. They stopped at a fast food restaurant and had some breakfast. They were anxious about Anna but they had both taken ecstasy themselves and couldn't understand why she had become so ill.

Neither of them, of course, had any idea of the multitude of ways a drug can affect the human system. The burr of George's mobile jarred their thoughts.

"I'm here by myself with Anna," Chloe told them. "I'm a bit worried. This doesn't seem normal."

"When we arrived," said Alexia, "Anna was on Chloe's bed. She had vomited everywhere except in the bucket. She was really sick."

The three of them sat with Anna for an hour. She seemed to be sleeping intermittently. "Sometimes she sat up and tried to throw up, but nothing came out of her mouth except spit," said George.

Finally he told Chloe to wake her mother, who was asleep in her bedroom. First, however, the three of them worked on the story they would give to Chloe's parents and, if necessary, to Tony and Angela Wood. "We made up this story about having her drink spiked at the go-kart track," said Chloe. "We did it because we didn't want Anna to get into trouble with her parents. We didn't know how bad she was. We didn't know she might pass away."

"We weren't scared for ourselves," said Alexia, sounding terrified. "We were very scared for Anna. We were so worried about Anna. We knew that if Anna's mum found out what she'd been doing that she would never let Anna see us again.

"I kept thinking: 'Oh my God, Anna's going to get drilled and they won't let us be her friends any more.'"

So they woke Chloe's mother, Judy, and said Anna was sick in Chloe's bed and that someone had spiked her Coke, possibly with drugs.

"We thought that would be okay," said Alexia.

Chloe's mother was startled to find a desperately ill girl in her daughter's bedroom. "She was curled up in a ball on the bed, facing the doorway," said Judy, "covered in vomit." She thought it would be too hard to find a doctor so early on a Sunday morning and said Anna should probably be taken to a medical centre.

"I think you had better tell her parents," she said to Chloe.

Finally obedient, Chloe went reluctantly around to the Woods' house and knocked on the door. There was no reply.

When she came back and told her mother that Anna's parents were out, Judy was exasperated. She was becoming increasingly concerned. She went across to the Wood house herself and knocked loudly at the front door.

18

SUNDAY MORNING

Angela Wood couldn't sleep. The visitors were long gone, the washing up was done. Tony, Alice and Julie were asleep.

Anna was just around the corner, in a house Angela could see from her window, watching videos with her friends.

It was such a shame, Angela thought, about those friends of Anna's.

She slid out of bed, went downstairs and found Saturday's *Sydney Morning Herald* untouched in the kitchen. She made coffee, sat down at the kitchen table and read for one hour and then another. She couldn't relax or explain why she felt too troubled to close her eyes and leave Saturday behind.

Exhaustion finally overcame her around 8 a.m., when she wearily climbed the stairs, lay down on her bed and slept at last.

A little later Alice woke up in her room, dressed and ran lightly down the stairs. She was "dog-sitting" for the people who lived opposite. Alice let herself out the front door and went across the road.

It was a clear but overcast day. Alice let herself into her neighbours' house and, after feeding the dog, settled down to watch *The Great Gatsby* on video. It was one of the books she was studying for her English paper.

"Somebody ran past the window," said Alice. "I thought it was Chloe. I wondered why she was going over to our place, when Anna was over there."

Within minutes the same figure returned. Alice realised that it was Chloe's mother, Judy. A couple of minutes later Angela Wood ran past the window, heading towards Chloe's house.

"I knew something had happened," said Alice. "I just knew. For some reason, I thought: 'I'm going to kill George.'"

She rewound the video, put the dog on the lead and walked outside.

The doorbell rang at 10 a.m., waking Angela Wood from her long-delayed sleep. She went downstairs and found Judy standing on her porch.

"You'd better come," said Chloe's mother. "Anna's ill. There's something wrong."

Angela ran upstairs, pulling off her pyjamas as she went. As she threw on a T-shirt and some leggings in the bedroom, Tony woke up.

"Anna's sick," she said to him. "We've got to get to her." Angela raced out of the house, across the cul-de-sac and into the adjoining street where Chloe lived in a large two-storey colonial-style house.

Angela swept through the front door and upstairs into the bedroom where Anna lay. She saw a clammy, cramping waif, sweating and smelling of sick, delirious and out of control. Her hair was matted with vomit and she had wet herself – her jeans were stained with urine.

For a fraction of a second, Angela Wood was angrier than she had ever been in her life. How had Anna allowed herself to get into this disgusting condition? Where had she been? What had she been doing?

Then she lifted her daughter into her arms and her heart exploded in terror. "It wasn't my Anna. It was as if someone else had taken over her body," said Angela. Her anger turned into horror. Her concern turned to fear.

"It didn't even look like Anna. Everything about Anna had been so perfect."

The two women began pulling the sick girl off the sodden bed. "Come on, darling," said Angela firmly. "We're going home."

As the two women dragged Anna out of the bedroom, Angela saw her daughter's three friends hovering at the back of the room.

"What have you done to her?" screamed Angela. "Where have you *been*?"

"It was a drink she had at the go-kart club," they gabbled. "Somebody must have spiked her drink."

They then all heard Anna's voice, slurred and sick. "What are you doing?" she mumbled. "Where am I going now?"

She didn't speak again.

As the two women reached the top of the stairs Anna collapsed, pitching forward and hitting her head on the door jamb. She slumped against the wall. Angela stared at her daughter, then whirled back into the bedroom and faced the three cowering teenagers who had been her daughter's closest friends.

"What has she *had*?" she screamed. "What have you been doing? You've got to tell me. She's *dying*!" They didn't answer.

Judy rang for an ambulance.

Angela took Anna by the arms and Judy grabbed her legs. She was now a dead weight, but they tried to carry her down the stairs, one step at a time. Halfway down, Anna's foot became jammed and they could move her no further. At that moment, her father came through the front door.

Tony Wood had risen and dressed in confusion; he'd been looking everywhere for the keys to Angela's car. He had it in mind that if Anna was ill, she would need to be driven to a doctor. He drove the car around the short distance to Chloe's house.

The sight of his lovely girl white and unconscious, sprawled across the stairs, stilled his heart.

As he came up the stairs to help his wife, she called a warning. "Don't pull her," said Angela. "We might break her ankle."

Chloe's mother rang a second time for an ambulance. This time ambulance officers gave her instructions over the phone and she relayed them to Angela and Tony. Anna was disentangled from the stair railing and placed on her side, with her knees up, at the foot of the stairs.

Tony was attempting to keep Anna conscious. "Don't die, darling," he whispered. "You have to keep breathing. I want you to keep breathing."

Panic was now gripping the small group at the bottom of the stairs. They felt rather than knew that Anna was in a state of respiratory arrest.

She seemed to have stopped breathing. Her life was flickering away.

In the distance, they all heard the siren.

"I could hear the ambulance coming for so long," said Angela. "I felt as if we were all in some other world and the ambulance was outside and too far away. It seemed to take an eternity to get to the house."

But it came at last.

Two ambulance officers attended to Anna, who now lay supine on the floor of the foyer. A second crew arrived to assist. They asked Judy to take the other girls out of the way.

"The ambulance people were very quick, really, and very efficient," said Angela. "They tried to revive her with their equipment. But they had to take her away."

While the ambulance officers carried Anna out to their vehicle, Angela ran home to get her bag and the necessary paperwork. Alice was just emerging from the opposite house, holding the dog by the lead.

"We're just taking Anna to the hospital," Angela told her elder daughter, trying to sound calmer than she felt. "She's had a drug overdose. Somebody has spiked her drink."

"No, Mum," said Alice, without understanding why her instincts convinced her that this wasn't the case. "That's not true. Those kids have given her drugs. They'll know what she's had. Ask them."

Angela stared at her daughter. "They said they don't know anything about what's wrong with her."

"Bullshit," retorted Alice. "Those kids take drugs every weekend."

Angela heard the truth from her daughter and had trouble taking it in. It was as if Alice was speaking a foreign language. She stared at her, mentally groping for the meaning behind her words.

"Why didn't we know?" she finally asked. "Why weren't we told?"

"Because it's just not the sort of thing that parents know," said Alice.

Anger stimulated Angela back into action. "Right!" she said, suddenly crisp and sarcastic. "Thank you for that information, Alice. We're just getting the car now and we're taking her to hospital. When she's better we'll talk about this."

Alice wanted to go to the hospital with her parents. Angela said it wouldn't be a good idea. "It probably won't take long but it won't be very pleasant," she said. "Anna will probably just have her stomach pumped. You stay here with Julie."

Alice felt helpless. "I didn't know what to do. I had the dog on the lead and I had the videos under my arm. So I walked down to the shops to take the videos back."

For a while Alice walked in numb fury along the footpath towards the shopping centre. Slowly she began to cry. "I was so angry. I was so angry that they had let it happen to her.

"I saw people I knew while I was walking. I saw a teacher from my school. None of them said anything. None of them knew what had happened." As Alice lived through the first minutes of her tragedy, it seemed strange that everyone she passed did not realise that her sister was suddenly desperately ill, that she was going into hospital.

"It's normally a twelve-minute walk to the shops and I did it in less than half that time. When I got to the top of the hill on my way back, I saw the ambulance. It was still outside Chloe's. They still didn't know what was wrong with her. They were talking about meningitis or a tumour . . . those kids were still lying about what had happened to Anna because they didn't want to get into trouble."

Julie was in the shower when she heard Angela run into the house. She hadn't realised she was up.

"Angela called to me that she had to go to the hospital with Anna," said Julie. "She said: 'I'll ring you later' and she went straight out again.

"I didn't know what was happening. I felt really nervous. I was alone in the house. Where was everybody? I just didn't know what to do."

With her stomach churning, Julie went outside on the patio to have a cigarette. Filled with a sense of foreboding, she began to cry. Tony found her there. The look on his face frightened her.

"Julie," he said hoarsely, "she's not going to make it."

Still ignorant of any of the preceding events, Julie stared at him.

"Who?" she asked.

"My baby."

"Not Anna?" she asked. Tony stared at her.

"You have to look after Alice," he muttered. "Find her and look after her for us."

Tony and Julie hurried outside and Julie began looking around for Alice as Tony went back down the street towards Chloe's house, where he had left the car.

Julie met Alice returning from the shops. Together they took the dog back and then returned home. Tony and Angela arrived back at the house as well. The ambulance was just leaving. Despite Tony's insistence that both Alice and Julie would be better off at home, Alice was desperate to go with her parents to the hospital. In the end, Tony said all four of them would go, and instead of taking Angela's car, they clambered into his van.

"It wasn't until we were in the back of the van and on our way to the hospital that I heard what had happened to Anna," said Julie. "But still we knew very little."

"We kept ringing those kids on the mobile all the way to the hospital," said Alice. "I rang them again when we were almost there. I spoke to Chloe, George and Alexia. I pleaded with them to tell us what she'd had. Alexia said she'd call us back."

Chloe's mother rang a short time later. Judy said her daughter had finally admitted that Anna had become ill after taking an ecstasy tablet.

"All the way to the hospital," said Angela, "I kept thinking we'd never get her back. I knew we'd never get her back the way she was."

Anna was taken to the Royal North Shore hospital. In Emergency staff worked on her for two hours before moving her to Intensive Care.

"They told us then they were pretty sure that her brain was gone," said Tony. "But they didn't give up. They kept trying. They did some tests. I suppose they were trying to find out what had happened. They told us there was no sign of any neurological diseases. The damage to Anna's brain was very recent."

A scan of Anna's brain showed that it was seriously swollen – she had massive cerebral oedema.

"We had to wait in a room for families," said Julie. "I don't know how long we waited there. Then they said we could go to see her.

"There were tubes everywhere. She was connected up to many machines.

"Tony couldn't cope with the terrible sight of Anna like that. He went out of the room. I gave Anna a kiss and left to see if Tony was all right. I hugged him and he said: 'I'm sure she'll be okay, Julie.'

"We stayed in the hospital all day."

"We went in the car to tell Sarine and Kathie what had happened to Anna," said Chloe. "I rang Mum up from George's car and told her to tell the doctors that Anna had taken a full E on her own account."

"By then it was too late," said Alice. "The doctors said they thought Anna only had a few hours to live, because her brain was in a lot of trouble."

"They had a little cemetery at the hospital," said Tony. "Angie was there, crying and screaming. I was in another direction and Alice was somewhere else. We were all so distraught."

Alice, Julie and Tony went home that night, but Angela remained at the hospital. Alice sobbed herself to sleep. Tony said he had never heard such a terrible sound.

Julie sat up all night in a large chair in the darkened living room. "I was really worried for Alice. I thought if she woke up someone should be there. I stayed up so she would have someone to talk to if she needed to."

In the early hours of the next morning Tony came downstairs. "Is that you, Julie?" he asked. He was surprised to find her there.

19

MONDAY

They returned to the hospital on Monday morning at 6 o'clock. Anna had been bathed and Angela had combed her hair. Anna looked peaceful. She was clinging to life. The family felt a flicker of hope. Another scan was ordered.

"We felt really bad that we had given up on her the day before and now it was possible she might live," said Alice.

"The kids all started coming as soon as they heard," said Chloe. "We had fifty people here at our house. They came every day, to talk, to listen to music, to pray, to be together. They brought food and photos of Anna. We were all waiting for news.

"My parents were really great. Dad went out and got them all food. Even when they had to take me to the police station to make my statement, they let all my friends stay. They trusted them."

"Everyone was bringing food and music and home videos of Anna to Chloe's," said Alexia. "There were people there all the time, in the house, in the yard, on the road, sitting in the gutter. They said Anna was going to die.

"I couldn't handle it. My boyfriend took me away in his car. We just drove around."

During the day, Anna's condition deteriorated. She was clearly unable to breathe without the assistance of the ventilator. There was one last test, a cerebral angiogram, to be carried out. It showed that Anna's brain was still severely swollen and that there was no blood flowing to the brain.

"It was just too big," said Julie, "there was just too much damage."

The family was told that there was no longer any hope that Anna would live.

"They were very frank," said Julie. "They explained everything to us. Anna was brain dead. Angela and Tony had to talk about whether they wanted Anna's organs to be donated. They also decided to invite Anna's friends to come and see her for the last time."

A list was prepared. On it were the names of the people the Wood family felt they couldn't face. These people were to be kept away from the hospital.

Angela came home with the others that night, showered and changed and returned to the hospital where she spent another long night with her strangely silent second child.

20

Tony, Alice and Julie returned to the hospital early.

The paperwork for organ donation had to be dealt with. Then, while Tony, Angela and Alice remained beside Anna, other members of the family and many of her friends began arriving. Through a horrible misunderstanding, Alexia arrived at Chloe's that morning and was told her name was on a special list of people who had been invited to see Anna.

"My boyfriend – we've broken up since then – he drove me to the hospital," said Alexia. "I ran in but the first person I saw was Anna's sister, Alice."

Alice was in the hospital corridor, trying to use her father's mobile phone. White with fatigue, worn out by tears, her nerves stretched to wire, she saw Alexia rushing towards her.

"What the fuck are *you* doing here?" screamed Alice. "You're a killer. You murdered my sister. *Get out*!"

Alexia turned and ran.

"There's a chapel in the hospital," whispered Alexia. "I went there. I looked at the cross and cried and cried. After a while my boyfriend came and said it would be all right and we went back to his house.

"Alice was upset with me because on the Sunday that Anna went to hospital, I'm supposed to have said to Alice that Anna never liked her, that she loved her friends more than her family. I

175

don't remember saying that. I asked if anyone heard me say it and nobody did. Only Alice.

"Later Alice phoned me and said I had to tell the lady police investigator the truth about where we had got the ecstasy. I was really worried about it. Alice said to me: 'Stuff you. You've stuffed up everything for my sister and me. How can you be so selfish? Go to the police and tell them the truth.' So of course, I did."

"They let me go to see her because I had told the truth," said Chloe. "The Woods weren't happy with Alexia and George because they hadn't told the truth at first. It's bad for George that they feel so angry with him because he is not a bad person. It wasn't his fault. It wasn't anyone's fault. Anyway, they just weren't allowed to see her."

Angela watched the people come and say goodbye to her daughter in a haze of grief and exhaustion. Old friends were there and new ones. Anna's close friends came, many of them with their families. Tears ran down their faces. Disbelief, confusion, anger, frustration, sorrow and incredulity ranged across their faces. How could this still white child be that lovely, bouncing, talking, lively, vividly smiling Anna Wood?

"I never saw Anna again after the ambulance left," said George. "On Tuesday I was at home when a friend of Alice Wood's rang to speak to my sister. I asked her if she had heard how Anna was. 'Haven't you heard?' she said. 'She died five minutes ago.'"

The girl who had provided Anna with the ecstasy tablet was sitting in an interview room at her local police station when the officer in charge of the investigation told her that Anna had just been declared brain dead. She began to cry.

She was charged with three counts of supplying a prohibited

drug and one count of possessing a prohibited drug. A date was set for a court hearing. Then, unlike Anna, she went home.

On Tuesday afternoon Angela and Tony agreed that their daughter's vital organs – her heart, lungs, pancreas, liver and kidneys were to be removed for donation.

At 8 p.m. the family left the Intensive Care Unit after Anna had been wheeled away for the final operation. The hospital staff suggested they should return about 2 a.m.

21

WEDNESDAY

In the early hours of the morning they saw their daughter again, but she was no longer the Anna they remembered. "She lay there like stone," said her father. Anna Wood, a girl as golden and warm as a sun-ripened peach, was cold.

When the family arrived home on Wednesday morning the media were waiting.

"The hospital had been really good. Nobody was allowed to see us while we were there," said Alice. "Nobody was told anything. The media didn't really know who Anna was or where she was from. Then they found out she had been at Forest High and they'd managed to get some of her friends to talk to.

"When we got here the whole cul-de-sac was filled with television vans and cars. There were cameras and lights everywhere, and people shouting and calling us."

Tony Wood said he would have been upset if the media hadn't come. He was eager to speak out against the proliferation of drugs which had brought about his daughter's death.

Alice, however, was appalled. "They were like vultures. They were nice, but they all call out at you: 'Talk to me! Talk to me!' They call you by name, as if they're old family friends. They followed us into our house. They tried to get into her bedroom, to see her things. I told Mum to stop them. It wasn't right. I've never been in a situation like that. I didn't know what to do."

A sympathetic neighbour, a public relations man experienced in dealing with the press, advised Tony that the only way to take control of the situation was to make a statement. The man was Chris Thomas, the communications manager for the Australian Medical Association. Anna used to baby-sit his three young children.

The dazed and grief-stricken little family agreed to a press conference.

Mothers and fathers all over Australia learned that a pretty, impulsive, fifteen-year-old schoolgirl – a healthy, happy child from a loving home in a pleasant suburb – had taken a designer drug at a dance and died.

The patience of parents across the nation finally snapped.

The battle for the life of Anna Wood was over.

The war was just beginning.

22

THE AFTERMATH

Down, down, down. Would the fall never come to an end?
(*Alice in Wonderland*, Lewis Carroll)

If Azaria Chamberlain had lived she would have been the same age as Anna Wood. Anna survived Azaria by fifteen years, but her sudden, senseless death upset and divided the people of Australia in a similar way.

This was no rejected street kid who took drugs to escape from the reality of a homeless, hopeless future. Anna Wood wasn't an unemployed delinquent or a runaway. She came from a comfortable home in a pleasant northern beaches suburb. She had just left school and secured an apprenticeship for the sort of job she'd always wanted.

Nor did the dysfunctional family factor apply. Her parents were happily married and reassuringly contented with each other and with her. Sibling rivalry? Her sister, Alice, was smart, popular and beautiful. But then, so was Anna.

Nobody wanted to believe that such a horrible thing could happen. Parents wrestling with the problems of rearing adolescents didn't want to believe this could happen to *their* children. Sophisticated young ravers didn't want to believe it could happen to *them*.

A wave of denial swept across the country.

In 1981, people could not understand how a little baby from a perfectly respectable middle-class family could be taken by a wild dog in the red heart of Australia. Nobody wanted to believe that such a horrible thing could happen. So they shot all the dingoes they could find and then put the baby's mother on trial.

In 1995, Anna Wood, her parents and her sister were subjected to trial by public opinion. People said they were . . . rather odd. They were so public about their daughter's death. They seemed so calm. They didn't scream and cry and sob – well, not when anyone was watching them. They kept talking about it to the press. There was Anna's funeral on the television, with the Woods marching hand in hand to the church, amid brilliant fans of flowers and sobbing rain. There were all those crying kids, wearing badges bearing Anna's smiling face and the message: "Say No to Drugs". As one newspaper reporter pointed out, after the funeral a lot of them lit up cigarettes.

They say it was an open coffin and Anna wore a red dress. It wasn't . . . discreet. Sure, the mother's face was ravaged by grief and Tony, the dad . . . he had the saddest eyes. But still you kept hearing from them. When would they go away and privately mourn the child they'd lost so that everyone else could put the whole horrible business out of mind?

Ecstasy users, determined to believe that their drug was safe, made up stories about Anna being on heroin; they claimed that she took too much E, that she didn't know how to use it properly, that she was already ill, that she was allergic, that she had meningitis – anything to justify their continued use of the drug. They didn't want to believe that anyone could die from just one ecstasy pill, so they made up fantasies that fitted in with their own experience.

Public and private debate about why Anna died raged for months. Some of it was moderate and responsible; most of it was hysterical, biased and based on rumour and innuendo. Some of it was spontaneous; much of it, in the courtrooms and in the press, was manipulative to an extreme degree.

They said she was a naive schoolgirl who had no experience of drugs until she took ecstasy that night (wrong); that she and her sister were hardened drug dealers (wrong), who were known to everyone in their local sleazy underworld of users (wrong). They said she was an invalid with an incurable brain disease (wrong), that she had actually taken heroin, not ecstasy (wrong), that she had taken twelve ecstasy tablets at a time (wrong), that she'd had an allergic reaction (unproven but unlikely), that she had mixed the tablet with other drugs (wrong). They said she had not died because she took ecstasy – and that was wrong. They said her friends had ignored her when she was ill (wrong) because they wanted to stay and dance (wrong) and she had died of their neglect. (Would Anna have survived with more prompt medical attention? Possibly, but we will ever know.)

Others have suggested that Anna Wood was ignorant about the potential danger of taking ecstasy (right), that because her friends were regularly experimenting with drugs she had no trouble obtaining ecstasy (right), and that when she became ill after taking the drug, her friends had no idea how serious the situation was (right), or how to help her (right). They did what they hoped was right, but in their fear and ignorance of the dangerous concoctions with which they were playing, their main objective was to keep her (and no doubt themselves) out of trouble.

That's what children do when they get into strife. That's what kids have always done. On the other hand, it's only in the past twenty years that children have had access to mind-altering chemicals – and a form of trouble they can't come close to comprehending.

The young people who said Anna Wood had taken ecstasy that night because she wanted to break out and have a good time were right. The old people who said Anna would be alive and well today if she had not lied to her parents and disobeyed them by taking illicit drugs – they were right too.

Yet these two views, however right they may be, are even sadder than the incorrect claims. Why does a fifteen-year-old girl from a happy home need to poison her brain to have a good time? Why was access to that poison so easy?

And while parents everywhere will support the view that children who don't do as they are told are sure to come to grief, disobedience in children is not usually punishable by death. At least, not in our society.

State high schools, and The Forest High in particular, came under fire. People said all the kids at Forest could obtain drugs freely and without fear of detection. This angered the hundreds of students at Forest who did not use illicit drugs, and upset the teachers who were proud of the school's excellent academic record. It also made all the high school students around the country laugh their layered heads off. They knew that drugs were available from certain sources in every sort of school, from posh private ones to local high schools, from convent schools to exclusive colleges. Police say there is a drug problem in every socio-economic district. Those girls and boys who wanted to experiment with illicit drugs – and it's important to remember that at the time of writing they were still a minority – knew who to ask and where to go. It wasn't hard.

Following a post-mortem examination, the New South Wales Coroner's Court initially announced that Anna had died from hypoxic encephalopathy or lack of oxygen to the brain. In simple terms, she had stopped breathing. It was *why* she had stopped breathing that was of interest both to the medical profession and the public, but this wasn't clear. Forensic scientists and toxicologists in Australia and England continued to investigate Anna's death and a final report from the State Coroner was withheld until a definite explanation could be made.

This didn't stop the people and the press from guessing.

Conjecture, rumour and gossip about the reasons for Anna Wood's death were fanned by ignorance. The papers had a field day with the story. People kept saying something had to be done to save children from drugs. But what? How? Who would lead the way? Whose problem was it anyway?

THE DEBATE

Two separate views emerged. Some people – medical professionals, academics, experienced youth workers, parents – suggested that the entire community needed much better education about the factual dangers of drugs and the foolishness of experimentation. They advocated stronger penalties for drug trafficking so that children – and, indeed, adults as well – could be convinced of the need to limit as much as possible the use of illegal drugs in our society.

The only solution, they said, was the no-drugs solution.

Angela and Tony Wood were prepared to lead the way.

Other people – medical professionals, academics, experienced youth workers, parents – suggested that children should be warned about the dangers of drugs, but taught how to use them safely if they chose to defy authority. This solution is called "harm minimisation".

A more controversial view in the drug debate is that certain drugs of abuse should be decriminalised. The most extreme view is that all drugs should be legalised.

Decriminalisation in Australia is usually the term used when possession and use of small amounts of specific illegal drugs are no longer treated as a criminal offence in the justice system; drug offences are punished with on-the-spot fines and offenders don't have a criminal record. Decriminalisation is also referred to as "expiation".

Legalisation of drugs means allowing them to be sold without reasonable restriction.

Advocates say these measures would ensure "quality control", reduce the "glamour" of illicit drugs, cut down on associated crime and defuse criminal networks which rely on the illegal drug trade for their profits.

No government in the Western world supports these proposals.

According to John Malouf, President of the Australian Pharmacists Against Drug Abuse: "Harm minimisation is like achieving 'Peace in Our Time'. Who could possibly oppose it?"

However, said Mr Malouf, harm minimisation applies to people already using drugs and should not be sent out as a message to children or young people who have not started and do not intend starting to use drugs.

"Of course kids should be told what to do in an emergency situation," said Mr Malouf. "They should also be taught not to accept drug-taking as normal behaviour. If we do that we are writing off today's young people as the 'lost generation'. It would be terrible for our kids and for the future of our civilisation if we just threw in the towel and gave up."

Telling children that if they must take drugs they should do it sensibly is practical advice, although it must be the saddest solution imaginable. As there is nothing "safe" or "sensible" about drugs of abuse, it is an admission of defeat.

"Quality control" means controlling the strength of drugs and making sure they contain the toxic substances from which they are alleged to be made, rather than a mixture of unknown chemicals. "This may be effective to a degree," said Mr Malouf, "but we have been led to believe that the real problem comes from all sorts of material with which the drugs are broken down. Because of this, many people assume that the drugs themselves are non-toxic, when the opposite is true."

While nobody has yet proposed that drugs should be available to children, the claim that drugs would be less appealing to adolescents if they were legalised suggests that young people would have access to them.

South Australia and the Australian Capital Territory have introduced a policy of expiation relating to cannabis, permitting minor offenders to be issued with on-the-spot fines without being convicted.

According to police, apprehension of drug offenders has increased in South Australia since expiation was introduced in 1987, as have drug-associated road accidents. Whether marijuana use has increased in South Australia and the Australian Capital Territory as a result of decriminalisation is open to further debate. A national survey conducted by the National Campaign Against Drug Abuse (now known as the federal government's National Drug Strategy) between 1985 and 1993 showed that during those years, marijuana use among fourteen- to nineteen-year-olds had increased from 28 per cent to 42 per cent in South Australia. However, the same survey found that teenage marijuana use increased at an only slightly lesser rate in Queensland, Victoria and Western Australia during the same period, with only New South Wales recording a small decrease.

Generally, government surveys among teenagers, following decriminalisation of cannabis in South Australia, have been described as "inconclusive". Eight years after such a ground-breaking decision, no wide-scale research into its effects – especially its effects on young people – has been carried out. Hundreds of thousands of parents would like to know whether their children would have been better off if the ground had remained rock hard.

An intriguing sidelight to the legalisation debate came from high school students in Western Australia, responding to the survey into drug use by Dr Peta Odgers.

"A lot of the older kids said they would not want to see marijuana legalised," she said. "If dope was legal they said they would be obliged to move on to something stronger, in order to maintain their reputation for being 'cool'."

Athol Moffitt, former President of the Court of Appeal and a New South Wales Royal Commissioner into Organised Crime, said removing controls on illicit drug use would be an absolute disaster.

"Legalisation would lead to escalating drug use with all the associated health risks, addiction and harm that they cause," said Mr Moffitt. "Organised crime would be greater, not less – and would target children, because for them drugs would continue to be illegal.

"The black market would continue; the illegal drug deals would be offered to the kids.

"Where would you draw the line? At what age would you let young people buy drugs? At fifteen? At sixteen? At seventeen? What drugs will you make it legal for them to buy? Just cannabis – the new variety known as Skunk, which is fifteen times stronger than the dope that was around twenty years ago? Will you include LSD, speed, ecstasy, cocaine, heroin, China White – a designer drug that killed one hundred people in California alone?

"How will you control drugs at dances and private parties? If they can have them at eighteen but not at sixteen, who will check their ages?

"We will never make any progress until we get rid of the propaganda that says drugs can be reliably used," said Athol Moffitt. "To win support, the pro-legalisation people have to convince us that drugs are not as dangerous as most of us already believe them to be.

"It's impossible to use drugs safely, as all of them cause some damage. It's like letting kids play with detonators – you can show them the bits that are dangerous, and you might save a few but you have no reliable way of knowing when they are going to accidentally cause an explosion."

John Malouf said he could understand why some health professionals who worked constantly with drug addicts were in favour of decriminalising drugs. They were much closer to drug abuse than most citizens and they could see little good coming from imprisoning the victims. However, he could also see why removing controls on drugs would not work in the normal community.

"It's a shame they can't remove the controls on drugs for three months, just to show everyone what a disaster it would be. You couldn't, of course, because with mind-altering drugs freely available, it wouldn't be safe for any of us to go out into the streets.

"This is the very reason why 104 nations of the world met in London a few years go and universally condemned the legalisation and decriminalisation of illicit drugs – a principle which is supported by the United Nations."

Mr Malouf said there had to be better education and greater reinforcement of the penalties relating to the drug traffic, if people are to be convinced how dangerous drug-taking is and that it cannot be condoned.

"If you drink and drive, you could lose your licence or go to gaol," he said. "The kids have got the message. It's a very dangerous thing to do.

"If you tip asbestos there's a $50 000 fine. We've all got the message. It's a very dangerous thing to do."

On 7 February 1996, the eighteen-year-old girl charged with providing Anna Wood and her friends with ecstasy was sentenced to 150 hours of community service and placed on a two-year good behaviour bond as punishment for her crime.

It was very hot in Sydney that day. There was no wind, but you could almost see the trees sway as a huge sigh of relief was breathed by all the drug dealers who were still selling their wares to their mates in cities, suburbs and schools throughout the state.

PARENT POWER
Unless we do something about the increasing rate of drug abuse very soon, Athol Moffitt believes vice and corruption will become as rife here as it is in third-world countries. Those who will suffer most will be our children.

Mr Moffitt has spent much of his retirement studying the effects of drug abuse in our society.

"There have been enormous changes in drug abuse in Australia during the past twenty years," he said. "Figures show that, along with New Zealand, we have the highest use of marijuana per head of population in the world.

"Marijuana use by people aged from twelve to sixteen increased 100 per cent between 1970 and 1990."

Australian figures have not yet equalled the 1979 record of the United States, which recorded the world's highest ever use of marijuana at 35 per cent of the population.

In that year, the parents of America decided they'd had enough. In a similar reaction to that which followed the death of Anna Wood, parents across the United States formed Families in

Action groups and set in motion a nation-wide campaign against drugs of abuse.

The political power and determination of parents surprised the government, but the American Congress took notice and eventually new laws against drugs were passed. Parent power worked.

Since 1980 the use of most illicit drugs has declined in the United States, and marijuana use has been reduced by 50 per cent.

"It was a long and difficult task for American families," said Mr Moffitt, "because a lot of groups still advocated the notion that drugs could be used without serious harm. But the power of parents turned the political tide in the United States, and in Sweden as well."

In Sweden the teenage drug problem has been well controlled by a huge community education program, where parents, teachers and young people have been provided with the overwhelming facts about the harm done by drugs. This has been supplemented with wholehearted support from the police, much stricter penalties for drug trafficking and effective rehabilitation schemes for drug users.

"While other countries are reducing illegal drug use," said John Malouf, "in Australia and New Zealand it is increasing so much that we now have the highest adolescent usage rate in any part of the world where records are kept.

"In New South Wales one in four teenagers has used an illicit drug. In South Australia it's one in two. In Sweden, where illicit drug use is down to a minimum, it's one in twenty."

Mr Malouf said a policy of harsh anti-drug laws but little education had not been effective in other countries. "It's more useful for our children to know the dangers that follow from the use of illegal drugs and why experimental drug-taking is foolish. They need to learn how to resist peer pressure, how to turn society's attitude towards drug use around.

"We should stop our kids poisoning themselves, but we have to tell them why."

TELLING CHILDREN THE TRUTH

There comes a stage in every child's life when they will no longer believe fairy tales. When it comes to drug use, parents have to tell their teenagers the truth, or risk losing their credibility.

Bob Budd, the Director of the Alcohol and Drug Foundation of the Australian Capital Territory, said parents who lied to their children about what drugs would do to them should not be surprised if their kids no longer believed anything they said and decided to find out for themselves – often at a high cost.

"Kids these days know they are not going to become addicts from trying drugs once or twice; they know they are not going to be lying in the gutter if they have a few drinks," said Mr Budd.

"Health education *must* be truthful. Parents have to give kids the correct facts and help them make sensible decisions. But if we go off the deep end with scare stories, if we try to deceive them, they may never trust us or listen to anything we say again.

"Of course we all face a real dilemma in that, by providing them with all the accurate details about drugs and chemical abuse, some kids who were never interested before may decide to experiment.

"Hopefully, on balance, it will be like immunisation – a very small minority may be harmed by preventive measures but, for the majority, it's well worth doing."

Young Australians are in the front line of the drug war. The seeds of alcohol, drug use and addiction are sown in adolescence. "If we could stop drugs being used by children in the twelve to seventeen age group," said Athol Moffitt, "we'd be halfway home."

"We will come up with a decent policy in the end," said John Malouf, "but how many kids are going to go down the gurgler before we do?

"Meanwhile, the second biggest market in the world is provided by the illegal drug trade. No wonder we've got a problem."

THE MISSION

Anna Wood's parents seemed to think their daughter's death was a problem that had to be shared. Rather than slipping sadly from the limelight, they kept talking about taking action to save children from drugs. Instead of hiding their grief away, they were brandishing it like a weapon – as if they believed they could bludgeon the drug trade into oblivion with the force of their pain.

It was too late for their own child but they were intent on saving others. They spoke to politicians, doctors, nurses, ministers of religion, academics, teachers, youth workers, newspaper reporters, television personalities and hundreds of parents like themselves.

Their hearts were broken but you never saw them cry. Some people thought it was strange and said so. They reminded each other that during her battle for justice, you never saw Lindy Chamberlain cry either.

But Angela and Tony Wood had more important things to do than to cry for the cameras.

23

THE PROJECT

"When I used to read fairy-tales, I fancied that kind of thing never happened and now here I am in the middle of one! There ought to be a book written about me; that there ought!"
(*Alice in Wonderland*, Lewis Carroll)

"When we came home from the hospital the last time, our first reaction was to close the front door and stay inside, away from all the press," said Tony Wood. "We felt as if we couldn't talk to people. We even discussed a private funeral.

"Then we saw we couldn't do that. It would have been terrible for her friends at school. They had to have a chance to mourn, to grieve. They were already sending flowers. They sent them to the hospital, to the house – there were flowers everywhere.

"We found we couldn't close our front door. The kids from Anna's school were all on work experience that week and they were wandering around in the streets, stunned, like lost souls. They wanted to come and see us. They wanted to say how they felt.

"They came in droves. They would trail up into Anna's bedroom and just sit there. Their faces – they were confused, frightened, they didn't know where to go, or what to do.

"There were kids everywhere in the house. The whole thing became very public.

"The kids didn't know how to talk to us, but Angie was great. She just hugged everybody. She's a really beautiful person, my wife."

When Ray Martin, a prominent television journalist and media personality, arrived to speak to the family, Tony had escaped upstairs. "I had reached a point where I couldn't cope and I had to go up and stay in my bedroom for a while. But Ray Martin was great. He has young children. He is as worried as the rest of us.

"The people who want to do something about drugs are all worried about their kids. Everyone is worried about their kids. Nobody feels safe any more."

"Our decision to get involved in drug education for teenagers wasn't a conscious reaction," said Tony. "It was something that grew out of the events that immediately followed Anna's death.

"The picture of Anna that everybody saw in the papers the day after she died had been provided by a company that takes school photographs. I don't know how the *Telegraph Mirror* got hold of it, I didn't want to read any papers that day.

"Then a relative rang to say how beautiful the photograph was. Thousands of people were seeing a picture of our daughter and mourning her death with us. So I went to the newsagency and bought four papers and in a funny sort of way the sight of her face was such a delight; it was wonderful to see this lovely picture of our girl.

"I think once we saw how the media were, that they were concerned, that they wanted to tell our story, we started talking to them. Everything snowballed from there.

"I can't say any of this has been easy for us. We could have put Anna in the ground and grieved in a back room. Instead we decided we would be better off doing something more positive.

"That's why we decided to become involved in the Anna Wood Drug and Alcohol Project."

When Anna Wood died, men and women all over Australia were finally struck by the magnitude of the country's youth drug problem; it hit home hard that not only neglected, homeless and disturbed youngsters were vulnerable – even ordinary children from happy homes were using drugs; one of them was dead.

No group was more horrified than the medical profession. Doctors, after all, are parents too.

Six months before Anna Wood died, the New South Wales branch of the Australian Medical Association (AMA) had made a decision to put its considerable human resources to work in the community, with an emphasis on helping the young.

In April 1995, the AMA (NSW) Charitable Foundation initiated its Youth at Risk program and began looking at initiatives which would alleviate the problems of youth homelessness, youth suicide and drug and alcohol abuse among young people.

Anna Wood's death, and the enormous amount of public interest and alarm which ricocheted around radio and television bulletins and featured in newspapers for weeks afterwards, provided a catalyst for the AMA's Youth at Risk plan.

Angela and Tony Wood and their daughter, Alice, were determined that Anna should not have died for nothing. At the invitation of the AMA, they met with members of the Foundation to discuss the possibility of salvaging something constructive from all that they had lost.

The result is the Anna Wood Drug and Alcohol Education Project, which aims to empower young people and parents to tackle drug and alcohol abuse.

With the support and assistance of the Wood family, the AMA has embarked on a national fund-raising campaign which will deal with the major problems of drug abuse among young people in this country.

The project is being run in co-operation with federal and state education and health systems, including private and public schools.

The Anna Wood project will differ from existing education programs in that it will hand responsibility for education to the young people themselves.

"The hardest thing to do when you are trying to educate kids about drugs is to get them to listen," said Foundation chairman, Dr Jack Burkhart. "They don't want to be lectured by some wrinkly who doesn't know the scene, who doesn't understand the way they talk or think.

"The obvious solution is that the right messages should come from young people who can communicate effectively with their peers and who are well informed and well trained."

Dr Kerryn Phelps, a member of the Foundation board, said it was important for young people to understand why they needed to avoid drugs; it was equally important for them to know the harmful side effects of drug and alcohol abuse.

"Like sex education, drug education needs to be scrupulously honest and unambiguous," said Dr Phelps. "It must reflect the experience of the young people themselves. Otherwise the whole message becomes impotent and irrelevant.

"We need to get high quality drug and alcohol education to all schoolchildren so that they are armed with the skills to avoid drug use."

One of the first steps taken by the AMA was the organisation of a Youth Forum on drug and alcohol abuse, which was attended by school students from all over Australia and chaired by Alice Wood.

The ideas presented at the forum were used to formulate the goals and objectives of the Project. One of the first initiatives stemming from the forum was a state-wide "Live the Future" campaign which took place in New South Wales in March 1996. With support from the AMA and the Department of School Education, students in hundreds of high schools ran mufti days, drug and alcohol seminars and creative workshops with the aim of raising funds for the Project.

Money from the "Live the Future" campaign is being used to develop a multimedia drug and alcohol education package, a unique CD Rom which will tackle the drug problem with material developed in close consultation with the students themselves.

Plans for the package include a video containing drug information presented by young people, and a computer game which will take players through the uncharted dangers of drug use.

Every school in New South Wales will receive a copy of the package for use in the classroom or library.

Tony and Angela Wood and the AMA also met with the Premier of New South Wales, Mr Bob Carr, the state Minister for Education, Mr John Aquilina, and representatives of the Department of School Education to discuss other ways the Project could be effectively piloted in New South Wales schools.

The goals of the Anna Wood Drug and Alcohol Project are:

- to establish a national drug and alcohol education resource centre to co-ordinate and produce information for school students, teachers, parents and the community;
- to establish a national training centre to train teachers to provide comprehensive and high quality drug and alcohol education;
- to ensure that, within two years, all Australian school students aged ten and over have access to quality drug and alcohol education.

To achieve these goals the medical profession, in conference with parents, teachers and students, have established the following objectives:

> • to establish a national grassroots campaign to counter drug and alcohol abuse among young people;
> • to educate young people about how to avoid drugs and the dangerous side effects of drug and alcohol use;
> • to ensure that young people are actively involved in national attempts to address drug and alcohol problems;
> • to educate parents on ways to effectively assist young people to tackle drug and alcohol issues;
> • to ensure that, within two years, high quality drug and alcohol education is provided in all Australian schools;
> • to address other issues of concern to young people, including problems such as youth suicide and youth homelessness.

The founding sponsors of the project are the Commonwealth Bank, Medical Benefits Fund and AAP Telecommunications.

"There are a number of reasons why the Australian Medical Association decided to become involved with this issue," said Dr Burkhart. "First, the death of Anna Wood catapulted us into instant action. It's a terrible thing when a young person dies out of ignorance. Second, there was a feeling among many of our 7000 members that it was time to get out there and contribute some of their experience to the community. When it comes to drug and alcohol abuse, the medical profession are among those to whom the community looks for leadership.

"None of us is going to do any good by wringing our hands and saying: 'Oh, isn't it dreadful? It's increasing all the time and we can't do anything about it.'

"We probably can't find a way to stop adolescents taking risks, but we *can* provide an effective drug education program."

Dr Burkhart said the Anna Wood Project did not offer a rehabilitation program for drug addicts. Rather, it is a preventative measure, aimed at "damping down demand" and decreasing the use of illegal drugs.

Chris Thomas, the Communications Manager for the New South Wales branch of the AMA, said Anna Wood had died needlessly. "She was a fifteen-year-old girl who took a designer drug. It doesn't matter whether she was a little angel or a little devil. It doesn't matter if it was the first time she took drugs, or the tenth time. The point is that she should have had better education. She should have been given more information about what she was putting into her body."

Mr Thomas said teenagers were experimenting with drugs at a much younger age than the previous generation. Telling them to stop was not enough. "We have to tell them why."

In order to do that, many parents, teachers and community leaders will have to learn a lot more about drugs. For parents in the nineties, ignorance is no longer bliss. Just as children cannot be taught how to deal with sexuality by pretending it doesn't exist, their mothers and fathers can't tell them to close their eyes and pretend drugs are not out there.

In order to make decisions, in order to make sensible choices, young people need information. For parents ready to learn, the facts are just a phone call away. (See Help Lines at the end of this book.)

For parents willing to listen, the kids have some ideas of their own.

24

SERIOUSLY COOL

"No room! No room!" they cried out,
when they saw Alice coming. "There's *plenty* of room!"
said Alice indignantly, and she sat down . . .
(*Alice in Wonderland*, Lewis Carroll)

At first they couldn't believe it. There was a party and they were invited. Girls and boys, school students, young people from every state – the kids were coming to town.

The grown-ups had finally admitted they needed help. Lots of help. And they were asking the children.

The teenagers would be talking to doctors, politicians, teachers and counsellors, all the adults whose work involved them in alcohol and drug education. Their views were going to be televised to the nation and published in books, magazines and newspapers.

People were finally ready to listen.

The students who attended the Australian Medical Association's National Youth Forum on drugs in December 1995, represented public and private schools from every state in Australia. Aged from fifteen to seventeen, they spent a day debating the issue of drug education and discussing recommendations for discouraging their peers from drug abuse. They then went home to try to put their ideas into practice.

Unlike many professionals confronted with the adolescent drug problem, these kids were not prepared to give up on their generation.

This is what they had to say:

"I think the main point that came out of this is that there's a lot of conflicting views from different people and there can't be a single solution because there's so many different circumstances.

"In general, both parents and children need to be educated a lot better about what's happening and children need to stop being afraid of telling their parents what's happening."

"A lot of the time it's teachers, adults and parents who put these seminars together and it doesn't relate to us. Out of my group, everyone wants drug education. They want the education in a way that we understand."

"I was talking to one of the television reporters covering this forum today and he had come from doing a report on a boy of seventeen who had just taken ecstasy. An ambulance was called as soon as this kid got sick and he was rushed to hospital. They thought he was dead but they managed to revive him, although now he's really ill in hospital. Luckily his friends went for help straight away.

"The point is that it's happening now. It's happening again and again. It's not just a problem that happens so rarely that people talk about it and then forget about it."

"I just want to comment on the sensationalism of the Anna Wood case and the amount of publicity it's got. There's something that really angers me – it's the way people want to knock it. Because . . . the most important thing is that it is being talked about. I didn't know the effect of taking ecstasy, neither did my parents,

neither did a lot of my friends. This case has caused everyone to talk about drugs and that's the most important thing . . ."

"This has motivated us to organise a special youth forum at our school. We are going for the shock tactic theme because we realise that actually works.

"We are going to get people from the rehabilitation centre who have alcohol-related problems to talk to us and also people who have been in car accidents because of drinking and taking drugs. We want to see the effects on them. We are going to spend time on body image and assertiveness and decision-making and things like that.

"When we said we were going to do this, have a Drug Day for the students, all the teachers got instantly defensive and said: 'Oh, we've done that already.' You know – 'There may be a drug problem in Orange but there's not one here.' That's just not true. You have to break through these barriers but, once you do, kids can make it work."

"A friend of mine died from drink driving. Shock value works. But I don't think it lasts that long."

"It's going to have to start in our schools but also there will have to be programs to concentrate on kids who have no homes and who have had no-one to love them. Because they will die and no-one will know who they are; already some of them have died of drugs and things like that. So I think there also needs to be something to reach them at the same time as we are doing it through the schools."

"There was a lady who came to our school in Victoria and told us how this boy who lived on the street was fourteen years old

and knew the effects of drugs. He deliberately overdosed on them, to die, because he was . . . sick of living. I think, like, it makes me upset and emotional and I think that when you are sick of living at fourteen, it is really sad."

"Talking about educating people at all levels, our school held a drug program for the parents of students at the school and . . . the school brought in doctors and people from the rehabilitation centres and all professional people to teach them about the problems of drugs . . . and I think it's a shame and almost naive of the parents that . . . only twenty people turned up. And yet, when the school holds an evening for how people are going intellectually, they get one or two hundred parents to turn up.

"That's something we've got to change as well. Not only teaching the students and people our age, but also making parents aware of the problem. Because I think they really don't know what's going on and the seriousness of the cause."

"Everybody seems to agree that we will go back to our relevant areas, where we live . . . and start doing similar forums to this. My suggestion would be that everybody works under the same title. If we spread that nation-wide, if we can start from every capital city and out to country areas, to where everybody lives . . . if we stay consistent and work together, hopefully something will get going from there."

"Once you've got a stable base in your school and made it known that you have an opinion, then maybe you guys can all start having an active role in drug education . . . What we've been saying is that we're not getting as much impact from older people coming in and telling things. If you can collect the information and support you need, you can then go to your headmaster or your co-ordinators at school with it, and see if they will let you run some drug education things. That way the students in your schools will have something that they can relate to, if they are listening to you guys saying it . . ."

"Our objectives are to get something national happening . . . We want it to be long-term; we want it to have grass roots, like make sure it's firmly implanted in everyone. It has to be pro-active, not reactive, like sort of preventative stuff.

"Students educate students, so basically the teachers don't really have that much to do with it, and maybe people might start paying attention. We need some sort of kit, so that we all have the same goals and objectives and are all implementing the same ideas, not going off on little tangents. We want to get AMA support . . . to get attention and make us look serious.

"We come from a small town and we need a name so people will take us more seriously. We have found that sometimes teachers tend to be defensive because they think it's just some dumb kids with some dumb project. If they recognise that there's a national group of us, united under the same objective, they might sit up and open their eyes a bit.

"Pick out the teachers that you know will support you and try and avoid the defensive ones. I mean, we did that; we picked out a teacher and he ended up providing us with transport, a thousand dollars in funding, and that's before we've even made a report on today."

"We need teachers because we need to get parents involved and if you don't get teachers' co-operation, a lot of the time the parents won't take any notice. What we were looking at was a national launch . . . we could have role models like actors and musicians . . . real people that you think are pretty cool. From there we could run it from our local areas, following national guidelines. It would be an ongoing thing and the suggestion was that quarterly we have a national forum again, to make sure everything's going okay."

"I go to a public school . . . and the teachers are too scared to teach us about those sorts of things, because otherwise we will go out and do it . . . that's what they think.

"But thank God my parents realised – you know, they'd done marijuana, so they realised what teenagers do. They've told me it's not a great deal. Things like that. *They* have educated me, not the teachers, not the school. I mean, a girl of fifteen started ecstasy here; a girl in Canberra, a sixteen-year-old, started heroin. There's got to be some education somewhere."

"It just seems to me that most of the teachers and parents work on the basis that ignorance is fear, that if we are ignorant about a drug then we're going to fear it and stay away from it. The thing with ignorance being fear is that, when you are actually confronted by a situation, because you are ignorant you *are* afraid. The trouble is that when a practical situation comes up you're afraid to go to the doctor; you're going to be afraid to go to your parents and you're going to be afraid to go to the hospital to deal with that sort of situation.

"I think that's wrong. I think we need to learn how to deal with our own situation and with other people's as well, because we are all different and we all need to be taught in different ways. Some people are saying: 'Oh, it would be good if we were shocked by something with drugs.' Other people are saying: 'Oh, shock value doesn't work. It doesn't relate to me.' The majority of people aren't touched by the drug education that's in schools now, because the broad range of education that you need to teach people isn't being used."

"We were thinking about actually setting up something on the Internet so we had our own address where we could put in what we were doing to get feedback from it and everything.

"There are a lot of different issues here and people have to deal with things separately and there's no one solution for everyone. We have to keep remembering that and not generalising, which has been the problem with our education so far."

"It seems people are just talking about drug education, dope, heroin, that kind of thing and what happens if people have an overdose. But a lot of people are forgetting that alcohol is far more prevalent in youth suicide and community costs than any of those drugs. There is just basically no education about that."

"I was in a situation just recently where my friend got really, really nuggeted and she was drunk . . . She's having all these problems at home and she was saying: 'Oh my mum hates me . . . blah blah blah' and then she decided she wanted to kill herself, so she was running around breaking bottles, trying to slash her wrists. I was totally . . . I was sitting with her trying to help her out . . . I just didn't know what to do. Her dad took her home in the end, but she was just so irrational that no-one could do anything. Everyone there was just acting like what she was doing was normal. Just: 'Ho, you're drunk' kind of thing."

"I don't think kids realise the effects of alcohol. They think they're going to have fun. They'll be sick the next day but hey, it's not going to affect them. It will be over in a couple of days. There'll be no major effects. Kids don't learn at school that it's going to affect them and they could do it again and one day it's really going to hurt them. They don't know of the numbers that are in hospital, after Friday night or Saturday night parties. People are just . . . ignorant."

"If your parents are, like, 'Oh well, okay, if you have a bit of a drink that's all right,' or 'Okay, it's your formal this weekend, you can go out and get smashed, that's fine' . . . I don't reckon they should be like that. But I don't reckon they should be total either, like, 'Don't do it.'"

"I feel that harm minimisation is a good way to go. If your parents say: 'Don't drink,' you're going to go out and do it. But if they say: 'Okay, this is the sensible way to drink. You can have three or four drinks and you will feel the effects but you won't be totally paralysed so that you don't know what you're doing,' that's the way to go. Teach kids how to drink sensibly. Give them guidelines."

"Educating parents about drugs is important and so is taking the glamour out of drugs. Maybe we could have a competition about the best way to do that."

"Keeping in touch with the kids who are in the midst of this problem at school is a good idea. We should have pamphlets available for people who want them – something that will be interesting and have an impact on students today, information material that won't look daggy or anything. You need visual creativity and involvement from . . . everyone in the school. One idea we had was to have a health awareness day . . . and it could be about all the problems that kids our age are facing, like drink, drugs, body issues and self-image."

"I think a wider range of education is the way to go. If you have been given plenty of factual information, you can weigh it up

when you have to make a decision. But the facts should be widely available because it might be two years after you've learnt about a drug that you are faced with the decision about whether or not to take it. Pamphlets with the facts about drugs should be around so that getting the information isn't a hassle."

"I think it's a little unreal using pamphlets. I know in Victoria we've got them and they really don't work that well. Are people going to come along and say: 'I'm going to smoke marijuana tonight, give me a pamphlet'?

"We agree that we've got to depend on our schools to teach us this and that, but I think a lot of influential people are your peers and parents."

"Most parents don't want to hear what you are going to do at the weekend because if they know they have to say: 'No, you can't go.' They don't want to hear the truth.

"Also, most people, including parents, drink and take drugs because they want to release the stress that's built up from school and work and everything."

"Whether you drink or smoke or take drugs depends a lot on whether you are a strong person or not. Some people are just naturally strong-willed and can say 'no'."

"We are not taught to have such self-confidence that we can go out for the evening and be ourselves and just be judged by ourselves rather than on whether we're drinking or not."

"I was talking to a girl who has never tried drugs and I asked her how she managed to get through that stage in life and she said: 'Well, I don't want to look really dorky and say I don't take drugs when I get offered them so I sit back and say no, I've tried them and it's really boring.' I thought that was a good idea."

"Like, be an individual! Like, I'm an individual – press that at parties. Like, don't make up excuses. Express what you want. And then people might start to look at you and say: 'Hey, maybe she's got a point; maybe it's the social cool to do that.' Yeah!"

Whether any of these plans and recommendations will be put into action is now in the hands of the AMA, the federal and state governments and parents and teachers across Australia.

The adults are now back in control. Advice from some astute young minds and compassionate hearts has been offered. Promises have been made. In the interests of giving the children of this country some faith in their future, let's hope they will be kept.

Yeah!

25

CHILDREN AND DRUGS: WHAT NOW?

Alice said nothing; she had sat down with her face in her hands,
wondering if anything would *ever* happen in a natural way again.
(*Alice in Wonderland*, Lewis Carroll)

They wear polyester as well as grunge, suits as well as denim.
They are men and women of all ages, of all nationalities. They
are dark and fair, fat and thin, tall and short, young, old and
middle-aged. They can be kids who look just like yours. They
can be parents who look just like you.

They are rarely men in overcoats with their hats pulled down
over their eyes. They may have swarthy complexions, dark
glasses, leather clothes and tattoos – or they may be clean-cut
brunettes in designer jeans and brand-name sneakers. They may
be women with waxen blonde hair, purple sacks beneath hollow
eyes and six earrings in each lobe – but it's just as likely they'll
be wearing clothes and jewellery you'd never notice.

Drug dealers are generally too clever to be recognisable by
anyone other than potential customers.

The only thing that unites drug dealers is that none of them
has a conscience about the unconscionable deeds they do. They
assume no responsibility for supplying drugs to people. They
believe – and there are educated, intelligent, responsible people
in the community who support this view – that responsibility for

drug-taking lies entirely with the person who knowingly puts that mind-altering combination of chemical substances into his or her body.

In a materialistic society where adult needs and adult greed always take priority, this may well be true.

But what about the children?

At what point in a young lifetime do we put a child in charge of her life?

Is it the first time she crosses the road without holding her mother's hand? Is it the first time he leaves his parents' home without them? Is it the first time she plunges out of her depth into the ocean? Or skis down a hill on her own? Or steps out onto a stage? Or rides a bike? Or falls in love?

Does a boy no longer need guidance because his voice leaps from a pipe to a drum? Should a girl child be independent because her body has begun to bleed?

Does smoking a cigarette, or drinking a beer, or screwing up his nose to taste champagne, make a child into an adult who is capable of making his own decisions about what he puts into his body?

Is a fifteen-year-old child who takes an illegal drug entirely and absolutely responsible for that decision?

If she dies, has she only herself to blame?

Who will answer? Who can tell us why?

THE POLICEMEN?

Detective Senior Constable Stephen Page, who investigated the death of Anna Wood, said teenagers are taking drugs in every suburb and town in the state and are not likely to be discouraged from doing so until those who influence them set a better example.

211

"Not only do they see adults drinking and smoking cigarettes and marijuana, they also read about their heroes experimenting with drugs," said Detective Page. "Naturally that tells them it's the cool thing to do.

"A lot of kids like to model themselves on sporting heroes, movie and rock stars and the young actors and actresses in the television soaps," he said. "Kids are much more likely to say no to drugs if the people they idolise and admire take a firm public stand against using them.

"If the opposite happens – if they hear their heroes use drugs, if famous young actors are dying from drug abuse and being caught with drugs on them – who can blame the kids for thinking that no matter how dangerous it might be, it's okay for them to take a risk too?"

Detective Superintendent Denis Edmonds, officer in charge of the South Australian Drugs Task Force, has been involved in a number of campaigns aimed at educating teenagers about drug abuse. He said the biggest question worthy of investigation was why teenagers needed to take mind-altering drugs at all. "Is it because life holds too much pressure for young people?" Mr Edmonds asked. "Or is it because life is not exciting enough?"

THE MOTHER?

Angela Wood believes our society has been mortally wounded over the past twenty-five years. Families, she said, have lost the plot. They have forgotten what life is really about.

"Why are we here? Why do we have children? Careers, success, material possessions – none of these mean anything if we don't value our children's lives.

"We have a moral obligation to the young people we've created and we've lost sight of it. The spirituality, the goodness that makes people respond to their children's needs, is dying out in this society.

"So many children don't have hope any more.

"People say: 'You'll never stop young kids buying drugs.' That's the easy way out. How do we know that if we don't try?

"Since Anna died we have had countless phone calls from people, parents and kids, who tell us who is selling drugs, and where and how. Many of the parents are desperate to save their children. But they feel helpless because so little is being done to stop the growth of the drug industry.

"Children aged twelve to seventeen are so vulnerable. Everything is changing for them. While their own bodies and emotions are in turmoil they are seeing movies and hearing and reading about experiences they have never had, about drugs which will induce feelings that will take them to peaks they've never reached.

"There is nothing for them to do, their parents aren't home, they are confused and concerned about the future. I can see why they are attracted to mind-altering substances.

"They are children. If there are people out there offering them lollies that will make them feel good and have a better time, can you blame them for wanting to take them?

"We have to give them help. We have to teach them what they are doing to themselves. We have to be there for them.

"It's a cop-out to say that both parents have to be out at work in order for a family to survive. For thousands of people whose kids are trying drugs, work doesn't mean affording a place to live and food to eat. It means material possessions.

"All we have to do is give some of them up, the way our own parents did."

"We neglect our children yet we do all that we can to help the people who provided our daughter and thousands of other people's sons and daughters with drugs. We forgive them. We have become

213

a nation of forgivers. So people die on the roads because drugged or drunken drivers are out there too. But we forgive them. So people sell our children drugs that can kill them or damage their brains. We forgive them. We punish them, but the punishments don't fit the crimes. They are fined, forgiven and set free.

"There is something wrong with a legal system that allows the victims of criminal offences – and children in particular – to be painted as the perpetrators of the crime.

"On Christmas Day 1995, while the dealers in death celebrated with their families and friends, our daughter's place at our table was empty.

"I know what the drug dealers and the people they are paying to defend them are saying about Anna. It suits their purposes to claim that she was a hardened drug user, an addict who was bound to get into trouble sooner or later. Suddenly Anna, one of many thousands of young victims, is being depicted as a law breaker who has only herself to blame for her death. Some people want to believe that, because it justifies her death, it takes away their own doubts and fears and guilts.

"Meanwhile, the criminals themselves, the people who are peddling death to our children, are being seen as the victims. The poor things feel so badly about what they have done that people are actually feeling sorry for them.

"I don't feel sorry for them.

"The people this family has to forgive are those children who were with Anna on the night she died. It has taken time, but we have asked them to come and talk to us. Their lives, after all, are still ahead of them. They have to be able to go on.

"Tony and I have been warned about speaking out too harshly about the evil people who sell or support the sale of drugs to Australia's children. There is a network of powerful and influential people out there whose interests are served by promoting illicit drug use in this country. We've been told that if we are not careful they could destroy us.

"All I can say to that is: Illegal drugs killed our daughter and destroyed the happiness of our family forever. What do we have left to lose?

"If I could have the last six months over again I would spend more time with my daughters and my husband. I thought I had always put my family first but now I realise how much I had let it slip away.

"But this isn't about our family any more. Anna, our most precious possession, is gone. The Anna Wood Project is about all the other children who are still here and who need hope. It's the responsibility of parents all over this country to put hope back into our children's lives."

THE FATHER?

"The kids here had a dance in memory of Anna the other night," said Tony Wood. "They danced their legs off without popping any pills.

"We've had cards and letters from all over Australia from kids and their parents. We've had hundreds of phone calls. We have a silent number but they still find us. Most of them are total strangers. First they tell us how sorry they are that Anna has died. Then they tell us what is happening to them. They're all so scared. They're worried about what is happening to this generation of children. They don't understand why they can't have fun without bending their brains.

"There are hundreds of mums and dads out there who don't know what to do. They don't know how to stop drug dealers. Nobody knows how because these people have been getting away with it for so long. They are people without consciences who are making a fortune. Why should they stop?

"Most of them are addicts themselves and because they are into it, they believe everybody else should be into it as well. If they were only destroying their own lives you could say it was their problem, not ours. But drug users don't just harm themselves. They are ruining lives. Children are getting hooked. People are being killed on the roads. Families are being broken.

"What's wrong is the number of doctors and specialists and academics who are misguided enough to want to legalise this stuff throughout the world. We want nothing to do with that idea. We don't support the legalisation of drugs in any way."

"It's now easier for kids to get drugs than to get cigarettes.

"A child, probably less than twelve, came up to me in the street the other day and said: 'They're still dealing, Mr Wood. The same ones are still selling ecstasy to people.'

"I said: 'I know, love. What can I do?'

"Some people think that kids from affluent suburbs like ours know what they are doing because they have so much education. It's not true. The kids have no knowledge about what these drugs are doing to their bodies and their minds. The more affluent they are, the more money they have to buy the drugs.

"It's fashionable. Binge drinking and drug-taking are supposed to make them cool. There are kids hanging around the shopping centres today, boasting that they are on the drug that killed Anna Wood. It's crazy.

"We've got to make it unfashionable to take drugs. We have to convince them it's not cool, that they don't need them. It's going to be a hard job.

"Working for the Anna Wood Drug and Alcohol Project has been better than locking ourselves away. We still grieve when we're on our own. I'm a very private person really. Angie has always been the one who gets involved in things like the school council and community affairs. I'm just a bloke who goes to work and then comes home and puts the dinner on. I really do enjoy doing that. It's what I miss most when I am away.

"The main reason I never got involved in anything before was because I thought I didn't have to. I was like all the other blokes who thought it would never happen to their kid."

THE SISTER?

"When you're Anna's age, life is all about risk," said Alice Wood. "People have told us not to smoke or drink or take drugs, so it's obviously a really naughty thing to do, so obviously we should try it.

"It's a bonding thing, too. You plan it and do it together. And it goes in stages. First you try cigarettes. Then you try drink. Then you try marijuana. Then some kids think that's pretty boring, so they try speed. Then coke. Then heroin. Some kids go up in steps.

"Perhaps some parents make the mistake of never talking about drugs to their children. They don't know any better because they don't know anything about drugs and when you don't know about something you're afraid of it. They think the problem will go away if they don't mention it. Or they are afraid that if they discuss drug-taking they are condoning it.

"In any case, young people don't take much notice of what the older generation tells them about drugs. Our parents talked to us about drugs quite openly, with little effect. What we need is young people who are the same age as we are, not talking to us so much as providing the right information.

"We want every school to have a small group which administers drug information. It would be like a student representative council. This group would be against drugs, but not to the degree where drug users were not welcome. They would just be

there to provide the facts on different drugs, to help kids understand that drug-taking is dangerous and could kill them.

"There will always be a percentage of people who will keep
taking drugs no matter what they know. But if we could
infiltrate the large numbers of kids who are doing drugs, if kids
like us could convince them that it's not necessary and that you
can die, that would be a 100 per cent improvement on what's
happening now."

THE WRITER?

After weeks of research into the adolescent drug problem, the
woman took an hour off to race to the shops and buy her own
fifteen-year-old daughter a birthday present – a CD of summer
hits which had been widely advertised on television and carried a
picture of a laughing girl on the cover.

It was good to be away from all those drug statistics for a
while, to look around at the crowds of noisy, healthy, jostling,
gawky kids, with their funny hair and sloppy clothes. It helped
to keep the drug issue in perspective.

The next day she went into her own daughter's room and
was taunted by the tuneless words that drilled from the new CD,
playing on the little white stereo on the frilly dressing table.

"Aah'm-on-the-drug, aah'm-on-the-drug, aah'm-on-the-drug,
aah'm-on-the-drug-that killed River Phoenix . . ."

Her kids were singing along.

THE FAMILY?

Following Anna Wood's unexpected death, a wave of teenage
confessions swamped parents living in her district – those bush
and beach suburbs which twenty years before had attracted so
many young families. However, only a handful of people were
blinkered enough to believe this was a problem exclusive to the

North Shore. In similar suburbs north, south, east and west of Sydney, in states all over the country, troubled parents started asking questions.

Anna's friends, Kathie, Chloe, Alexia and George, as well as various others, made a clean breast of all their activities to their parents. Teenagers and adults alike admitted that the purging had brought them closer – that in the long run, it would probably do their relationships a great deal of good.

But what about the teenagers who have not been provided with such a tragic opportunity to break down the barriers between their parents and themselves?

Family life is being influenced and subtly undermined by certain influences which are at work in our society. The pressures of work and time are the greatest threat to the peace of family life in the nineties. However, families also have an image problem. Movies, media, social workers, counsellors and government reports too often regard the family unit as a seething nest of conflict and resentment, particularly when adolescent children are involved.

In actual fact, surveys by the Australian Institute of Family Studies and other national polls show that families are still the greatest source of happiness, relaxation and satisfaction for the vast majority of people.

This is true of most Australian families, no matter what their wealth or status may be, no matter how many children they have or what ages those children are; regardless even of whether a family involves one parent or two.

Because they provide the foundation for our society, because they have an enormous influence on the development of intelligence, competence, physical, mental and emotional health, vocational choices, morality and on the way people relate to others, families will never be peaceful and free from trouble. There's too much going on in them for that to happen.

Family life has its ups and downs, its hugs and brawls, its sulks and its celebrations. But whatever the basic shape of a family may be, nobody has come up with a unit that works as well.

For these reasons and many more, adolescents need to be part of family life. At this vulnerable stage of their lives, they need the reassurance, the interest and the love of their parents.

One of the saddest developments which has occurred in our society is the tendency for teenagers to leave home when life gets difficult. Holding their parents responsible for everything that is going wrong and assured of financial support from the government, some rebellious adolescents move out and live with their peers rather than their parents. If their claims about their parents' treatment of them are sufficiently serious, they need never submit to their authority again. In their youth and naivety, few of them realise that without that parental authority, real freedom and genuine maturity will be much more difficult to attain.

Parents who wish to maintain some control over their children's lives, safety, morals and behaviour feel threatened by the very real fear that if they even nag a little, they will lose their children.

There is no real solution to this problem under the current laws, which are in place to protect the rights of that minority of children who are abused and whose safety is at risk.

For the vast majority of loving parents, prevention is, as usual, better than cure. Keeping communication lines open from the beginning of family life is more effective than attempting to introduce intimate chats only when their bodies grow bumps. It's going to be hard work establishing a connection in puberty if the previous decade of conversations has been limited to: "Have you cleaned your teeth/washed your hands/tidied your room/fed the cat/done your homework?"

When children turn into teenagers, just saying "No" isn't enough. Just loving them isn't enough either. But then, it never was.

26

JUST FOR PARENTS

"Why did you call him Tortoise, if he wasn't one?" Alice asked.
"We called him Tortoise because he taught us," said the
Mock Turtle angrily . . .
(*Alice in Wonderland*, Lewis Carroll)

Kids have always taken risks. They always will. Kids have *not* always taken drugs. A majority of them still don't. To increase that majority it is essential for parents and their teenage children to discuss all drugs, and the way they can affect the quality of human life.

Too hard? The good news for parents is that it is almost never too late to do better than before. The bad news, which most of you don't need to be told, is that having an open and honest discussion with teenage children is not usually easy.

Communication is particularly hard. Adolescents are moody and unpredictable. Conversation is complicated by the fact that if they are high on happiness they haven't got time to talk and if they are low on misery they're too depressed to listen. Catching them in-between can take as long as crossing a six-lane highway – and is just as big a risk.

When the best time finally arrives, however, and the topic for discussion is drug use and abuse, be prepared. In order to tell children the truth, it's essential for parents to be in possession of as many facts as possible. Educate yourself first. Information about drugs and alcohol is available from hospitals and community health centres or, even more conveniently, from alcohol and drug agencies which will send you the materials you need. (See Help Lines at the end of this book.)

Regardless of their differing views on the difficult issues which arise from alcohol and drug abuse, all the professional and medical people who were consulted in relation to this book agreed on one vital principle.

The best thing parents can do for their children in the present climate is to acquire the essential facts about drugs and then bring the subject out into the open for family discussion.

HARD STUFF

- Talk about drugs. Name them.
- Talk about why people take drugs: To escape reality by getting "high"? To find relief from emotional pain? To reduce pressure, slow down, relax? As an act of rebellion? To challenge the limits of normal existence? For fun? To be "cool"?
- Talk about the negative effects of drugs – on health, happiness and life itself. Discuss this calmly and sensibly. Don't exaggerate. Don't lie.
- Talk about what to do in a dangerous or life-threatening situation which has resulted from drug-taking. This can range from not getting into a car with someone who has been drinking or smoking marijuana, to witnessing illness in a person who has taken ecstasy, LSD or speed.
- Acknowledge that many adults abuse drugs like alcohol and cigarettes but point out that this doesn't mean kids should make the same mistakes.

223

- Two of the oldest rules in the book are still valid for parents today. Set a good example. Practise what you preach.
- Establish the fact that you are trusting them to use the information you are providing wisely.
- Whatever decision they make, let them know they can always talk to you about it.
- If they then tell you they are already taking drugs, discuss their reasons for doing so with them. Suggest alternatives. Emphasise the negatives and make doubly sure they know about emergency procedures. *Stay calm!*
- Tell your children the choice is theirs. Make sure it's an informed choice.
- Drug education, like sex education, cannot be dealt with in a one-off, sweaty-palmed, no-holds-barred session. Return to your discussion at reasonably regular intervals, adapting your message to suit the development and maturity of your children.

HARDER STUFF

Drugs are only one of many pitfalls which trip up families on the rocky road through adolescence. Communication is the key to finding the smoothest way through, no matter what the issue may be.

Communication means listening as well as talking. It means answering kids' questions as well as asking your own. It may mean waiting patiently until they are ready to talk. It means trying to understand your young people's opinions without resorting to sarcasm and criticism.

Acknowledge that with the guidance and information you have given them, they have reached a stage where they have the right to think for themselves, not only about drugs but about many of the issues with which they will be faced as a result of their increasing maturity.

Parents need not feel threatened by their teenagers' developing independence. Adults are still older and, in most cases, wiser. Listening to what your kids think doesn't mean changing the way you do – unless you want to.

- Be around. Not all the time, but a lot of the time. Be invisible but present at their parties and gatherings.
- Keep them busy and involved. Encourage sport, youth groups, projects, picnics, walks, dancing, music, safe risks.
- Be tolerant of their strange appearance, clothes and music, but be honest and true to your own tastes. You don't have to become one of them. That's the last thing anyone wants.
- Encourage them to talk – not just about the controversial stuff, but about anything and everything. Ask them about their day. Ask about the magazines they read, the rock groups they like (if you can't cope with the music, ask about the children/marital status/natural hair colour of the drummer/base player/lead guitarist), the success rating of the movies they go to see. Ask their opinion on the ordinary business of life – should you plant a shade tree there? What do they think about moving the clothesline so everyone can play touch footy in the yard? Don't shut them out just because they've become big and hairy and alien. They are still part of your family.
- Ask them for their opinions. Listen to what they say. You don't have to agree with their ideas but you can respect their opinions. Acknowledge that they are not only growing, they are going – in spirit at least. As they must.
- Would you like to be a teenager in today's world? Give them sympathy and comfort.

- Laugh – with them, not at them. Almost everything is funny eventually. Sharing a sense of humour with kids, relating disasters of your own and chuckling with them over theirs, once the pain is past, can create the strongest bond of all.
- Above all, just be there for your teenage children. They need you more than you will ever know.

27

ANNA'S STORY

"I know I am only fifteen but I have a feeling my time on this earth is short and I suppose I should make the most of it!"
Anna Wood, 5 September 1995

Everyone who loved Anna Wood believed they understood her well. They did – and yet, they did not. Despite her open smile, her friendly nature and her direct manner, Anna was not always who and what she seemed. In that, she was typical of us all.

She was her mother's angel and her father's best mate. She was a silly, loving, considerate, nuisance of a sister. To adults she was a happy, loving child. To her peers she was a passionate, loyal, outspoken, happy friend.

She was mischievous, inquisitive and witty. She had a wicked sense of fun. Impulsive and outspoken, she was also intermittently vulnerable, depressed, worried about the future and full of doubts about herself.

Why did she risk her bright young life by taking the tablet that killed her?

Was it her insatiable curiosity? Her longing to do something different? An initiation into her new "grown-up" life?

Was she feeling neglected because her mother was working long hours and her father was frequently away? Was it a way of showing that she was taking control of her own life?

Had Anna become tired of always being a "good girl" – was she sick of counselling care and caution, especially when many of the girls who disregarded her good advice seemed to be having a better time?

Was it an impulsive risk resulting from boredom?

If it was lack of information, what about the conversations with her family, the facts she was given at school, her friend Chloe's drug-induced deterioration, her visit to hospital to see another friend suffering from the effects of amphetamines? Was Anna just plain stupid?

If it was peer pressure, why did each of her best friends claim that Anna could never be forced to do anything against her will?

Did it go deeper than the obvious – could it have been a painful attempt to block out the destructive feelings resulting from her sexual abuse twelve years before? Were the poems she wrote about it cries for help – or are they typical of the dramatics in which teenage girls indulge themselves?

In the end, did Anna take ecstasy just for fun?

Because nobody will ever know the answers to these questions, it would be presumptuous to attempt to write Anna's story for her. Instead, here is a selection of essays, poems and letters written by Anna in the last two years of her life.

Spelling and punctuation has been corrected where possible; otherwise each piece appears as she wrote it.

Only two letters mention drug use. By her own admission, and typical of the vast majority of fifteen-year-old girls, Anna's most consuming interest was boys.

Apart from the rhymes about her family, which are written with sardonic humour, Anna's poems tend to be bleak and gloomy. Her letters to her friends provide a striking contrast. Even when she was feeling down she expressed herself most exuberantly on paper – usually paper from the schoolbooks in which she was supposed to be working at the time!

Read them and weep. Read them and smile.

That's Anna.

ANNA BY ANNA

Always loved animals
Never liked cruelty to anyone
Never would hit an animal hard
Anybody who is cruel beware!

HELP! [A SCHOOL ESSAY]

It was a Sunday afternoon and Stacey was getting really nervous. Tomorrow was going to be her first day in Year Seven at high school.

"Mum, I feel sick, I can't go to school tomorrow."

"Don't be stupid," said her mum, "everything will be all right."

Mum just doesn't understand, she thought.

That night she couldn't sleep. Every time she dropped off she woke up again.

When the morning came her nerves turned into excitement; all she wanted to do was go. Well, eventually they got there and Stacey's nerves came back. The Forest High had a pretty respectable reputation but some people said that it was quite rough!

As she walked in the gate people began to stare at her and she began to be frightened.

Then the first bell rang and she went to her peer support group waiting at the assembly hall. Stacey knew

*that one of her peer support leaders smoked and she
was very against it, but she knew she couldn't do
anything about it.*

*Stacey's group went down to the middle of the oval
to write out their timetables and while they were down
there, one of her peer support leaders lit up a cigarette
and started handing it around. Stacey didn't know how
to say no so she tried it.*

*She coughed and she wheezed but no-one took any
notice and it was still being handed around and then it
came back to her again.*

*She rather liked it so she tried it again but this time it
was better.*

Dearest Kasmus [one of her best friends]

*Hey Smelly! Well, I am in art, sitting next to Sazzy
Wozzy who as per usual is being a good girl and doing
her work. Honestly, the Gangster Party is a SIK idea.
I'll bring the cards, cigars, whisky and myself. Actually,
maybe I'll skip the whisky and cigars and replace them
with vogues and bacardi.*

*Okay, what should we wear? Are we gangsters,
gangster girls, sluts, whores or nice guys? Leave the last
one out. Now I have three things to look forward to and
they are:*

1. Skiing. 2. Formal. 3. Kathie's sixteenth birthday.

*Picture this. It's the seventh of January and we are
already at your dad's, ready for the night to start. You
are dressed in a long black number with a red feathered
scarf and a diamond choker and shoes high enough to
commit suicide off, with fish net stockings. I am*

wearing a slinky red sequinned number . . . NO!
Stop that thought, better one coming . . . You should
have a flapper party. No, don't laugh, I'm serious.
The flappers were in the nineteen forties or fifties.
They wore tiny loose little dresses with sequins,
diamonds, the lot!

Oh well, I'm sure we'll have lots of ideas before the
special date comes around.

 Anna

WHAT I WANT LIFE TO BE LIKE

I wish life was as simple as pie,
Nobody doubting or asking themselves why?
People living their lives as one,
Arguing and fighting – NO. None.
No politics, no monarchy – the people rule,
If anyone steps out of line, make them feel like a fool.
But life is not like that, nor never will.
These days people go out at night just for a kill.
What I want life to be like is friendship all around,
And the feeling of love reach space from the ground.

Dear Bitch of Kascarde,

Hey dude, how's it flopping? Skiing is going to be a
cackle! I'm so excited, are you? Are you still waiting
for L? Guess what – I am growing my nails so I don't
need fake ones any more. Well, since you did my
favourite part of our letters, I have done one for you.
It's a QUIZ.

1. If you met another guy up at the snow and he was so sweet and hot (even more than L) and you had a chance to be with him without L knowing would you . . .

    (a) Be with him but explain it can't go any further?

    (b) Just go for it; L would understand.

    (c) Tell him where to go for a hike, you would never do that to L.

    (d) Not think twice; slap him and run.

2. You were at a Zillian concert and your best friend Anna (Bitch of Annasvala) was pissed. You were going to have the best night except for Annasvala doing that. You . . .

    (a) Dump her, she's not ruining your night.

    (b) Look after her and have a bad night.

    (c) Find someone else to look after her; you're not stuffing up this night.

    (d) Look after her for a few minutes, then go and have a good night; you've done enough.

3. Your sister was injecting heroin and she asked you to try some. You . . .

    (a) Think one time is not going to hurt.

    (b) Tell her she is stupid and walk away.

    (c) Sit down next to her and just watch.

    (d) Tell her you want nothing to do with her ever if she is that stupid.

    (e) Get a bucket of water and drop it on her head.

    (f) Tell her you would prefer her to do it in front of you than behind your back.

    ♡ *Anna.*

MUMS

Mums are something that we all need,
She puts food in our mouth when we want a feed.
If we didn't have a Mum we wouldn't be here.
We run to her if we have a fear.
Mums are the most fantastic people.
She fed me at birth with her neeple. (Sorry!)

DADS

Dads are like blue roses
Hard to find and hard to get
Or even like little birds lying in a nest
But I will always think that
My dad is one of the best.

FAMILIES

I love families for they are there
To love, to share, to care.
To never ever doubt
I love my family for they never SHOUT.
(NOT!)

Dear Alice [on the eve of her sister's departure for France],

I would never tell you this in person, but writing it down is easy. I suppose I will miss you but I think you will have the best time and won't miss us at all. It's a shame you're going to be away for Christmas and your

233

birthday, but I'm positive you will be having a better time over there than you would over here.

Think of us when you're away every now and then and even though you are only going for a couple of months it will seem longer.

Please say hello to everyone and give Flicky a big hug and kiss from me.

See ya big sis.

Lots of love, Anna

Dearest Real Mum [Mothers' Day, 1994]

This is just a letter to say I love you and you are the only Mum I really love. I know I have been a big pain lately and I am sorry. When I am doing it I don't realise I am but afterwards all I can say to myself is "what a brat!" I am really sorry about the way I have been acting but I can't change what I have said but I can TRY and improve!

If I have another tantrum soon remember I feel really bad but if we both try hard to get on there will be no problems.

I love you heaps Mum and I hope you have a WICKED Mothers' Day! I love you.

Love, your biological daughter, Anna.

CITY LIFE

You get to work in your miserable state,
Everywhere you go in the world seems in checkmate,
You walk to the window and look all around,
See the pollution stick like honey to the ground.
The world is in trouble you think to yourself,
People are coming selfish to reap all their wealth
The economy is breaking down, down, down,
Nobody can save this dying town.
Thieves are working everywhere,
People look at you with a cold hard stare.
Alone children are living in unusual places,
People are dying because of their races.
Graffiti is everywhere all over the streets,
Our landscape is ugly and not very neat.
You want to escape to a beautiful place,
Or even just one that has more grace.
This world one day will be totally black.
But there is one way we can turn back.
We should start looking after those less fortunate than we are
But getting the world back on his feet is a long job so far.

Dear Sally [a former schoolfriend in England],

How are you? We are having a big party tonight for Alice's return. So how has everybody been? I am dying to see the video Alice brought back just to see everybody's faces again. I have so many things to ask you and to tell you, but it's been SOOO long I don't know where to start.

Okay, first, how is everyone, I mean EVERYONE? How are the people from school and the people at the pub? Are you and Jill still best buds? Say hello to her for me. Sorry to dump all the questions on you, but there's still one more – who is the love of your life at the minute? Anyone I know? My love life is at a standstill at the moment. I can't make up my mind. No, actually I think I'm just in for the chase. When eventually I DO get one I keep flirting. I don't want one any more!

I have made some really nice friends over here and I am really happy. I love school – actually I hate school. No, it's all right. I am on holidays at the moment and it's great. I am unfortunately unemployed at this point in time, but with a little luck, I might get a job in a boutique in Manly!

I'm in to all music except heavy metal. I hate that. I especially love techno. I just can't get enough of it. I used to hate it, but my tastes have changed. What about you, what sort of music do you like?

I really miss you all heaps and am dying for the day when I see you again. Please keep in touch.

Lots of love, Anna

WHAT GAVE YOU THE RIGHT?

I wonder if you can remember what you did
What you did to me when I was a kid
I wish you thought before you touched me,
You've locked up my heart and stolen the key.
Why did you think that you had the right
To touch a child when she was too young to fight?
I sit there at night crying and think what you've done,
But at least now I know you have not won!

[ON THE SAME THEME]

Dirt, disgust, guilt and betrayed
Someone has stolen your soul; it's not a game
Years after people think you would have forgot
But their touch will always be with you.
You try not to think about what has happened before and wish
life would go on.
Child abuse is something not many people think about but it
will always be in the mind of the victims.
Why would someone do something like that, you may ask
yourself, but that question is one that nobody can answer.

Dearest B . . . [male schoolfriend],

How are you, my violent sex partner? Well obviously today's PE lesson is going to be a boring one! Well, as I said, I am not any good at writing letters and so I just babble on about everything and anything. Oh oh, I think my pen is running out!

New pen! I was not allowed to write to you in PE on
Wednesday, so today is Thursday and I am in Science!
We are doing chemistry and it is sooo hard! We just got
told that we should clean our houses with urine! How
gross. Have you got any plans for this weekend? I have
a feeling this weekend is going to be boring – Friday night
hopefully I will do something but Saturday night I have
to baby-sit. BUT Sunday is going to be SIK! Manly vs
Norths and I will be there! Manly will kick ass! What are
you going to do this weekend? Sorry, I just asked you that.
  Anna.

Dear Mamma,
  Happy birthday. I'm sure you already know this but
it's always nice to hear this again. I love you very much
even though you're nearly an old fogy (just jokes).
  Have a fantabulous birthday.
  Lots and lots and lots and lots of love, Anna.

Dear Kath,
  I just wanted to tell you before this gets out of hand
that the reason I got so angry was because I thought you
just sat there and took what Z was saying. I don't know
whether you stood up for X or not but if anyone ever
called you a slut to me I would knock their blocks off
and that goes for Alexia and Chloe too. I am sorry for
getting so hyped up but I have just realised what all of
you mean to me – not that I didn't know it before!
But in the past couple of days I have just wanted to
tie you all up and carry you all around with me. I know

238

Z is your friend and I understand that you were just listening to a friend's problems but I don't like Z one little bit and I won't let her talk about any one of you.

I hope you forgive me and I love you heaps. But please try and understand why I got so angry. I also know X would stick up for you because she has done it before.

I'm sorry sweetie. I will always wrap you up in cotton wool. I hope you will do the same. Do you forgive me? Yes? No? I have to learn to keep my anger under control.

Love ya ♡ Anna

FRIENDS

If you ever need someone to turn to
Your friends will always be there for you.
You will sort things out day and night,
Although you may sometimes seem to fight
You will go through a lot, you and friends
Although you may sometimes tend
To fight and sob and laugh and cry
And when you fight you may ask yourself why?
Why you were so stupid to nearly lose
This friend that you had to choose?
And always remember that you and your friend
Will always work things out in the end!

FRIENDS

. . . Who needs 'em?

I FEEL

I feel the world's troubles fall down on my shoulders
I wish life was simple but I know it's not
Why oh why I ask myself, but
My heart's reply is none.
I want the feeling of self-doubt to go.
I want my confidence back.
What must I do to make things normal?
Or is the question: What IS normal?

31.8.95
Dear Shefa [her imaginary friend-cum-diary],

I made the decision today that I am going to do well in school. I know all the teachers think of me as a deadhead but for the first time in my life I have wanted to prove them wrong. I have never really cared what they think and I still don't but I do care about my parents and I know it will make them happy to see me do well at school. Not only that, I want to do this for myself too. Short entry but I still luv ya.

[And as a result, a contract:]
Contract

I Anna Wood have decided to try the best I can in school. I am going to whip the pants off a lot of good students in school. Not one piece of homework will be late and not one assignment will be not finished.

I am going to do my best.
Signed: Anna Wood.
Witnessed: Angela Wood.

Mr B! [note written to her maths teacher on test paper]
*I know I have done absolutely dreadfully in this test!
Do you think I should go down to General? I understand
it all in class but when I started the test I just lost it. I
even did study but I can't remember studying much of
that because I thought I knew it! There you go! Sorry!*

Dearest Kath,

*How RU Sweetie? Well, I just got into another fight
with Mum! We are always fighting lately. We always bif
when Dad comes home after being away for a while. It's
like she hates it when he's home and she knows how
close me and Dad are so she takes it out on me. I can
handle that but this time she's been bringing Chloe into
all our fights and it gets to me sooo much I just want to
scream! What should I do?*

(a) Kill her and get it over with?
(b) Ignore her for a while and see how she reacts?
(c) Let it pass?
(d) Make her insanely jealous by sucking up to Dad?
*I love the idea of having A&C folders, it's excellent!
Geeze I've put on heaps of weight – it's just I can't stop
eating, it's like I need heaps of food. Maybe I'm
pregnant. Could happen, virgin pregnancy is not
unknown – take Mary for instance.*

*How's your heart feeling about D at the moment?
Who do you think I like? . . . . (answer here).
If you wrote S you are wrong. If you pick wrong you get
a dirty look from me. If you pick right you get a hug
from me. Make sure you choose wisely, either way I'll
get you!!*

♡ *Anna*

Notice!

[Draft of a notice relating to the end-of-year school formal to be held in December 1995]

This note is just to remind the Year Ten students of The Forest High about the most exciting time so far in their high school life – THEIR FORMAL.

We are hoping to see everyone there to join in on one night of the year when all students combine.

The cost of the tickets is $50 which is quite a price but it WILL be worth it. We know that everybody will be on their best behaviour but we still need you to fill in the contract below. If any damages are made it will not only give a bad impression to the owners of the restaurant but it will make extra costs. Please don't let us down!

Contract: I will be on my best behaviour at my formal and will keep my maturity until we leave. I will NOT let my fellow students down. Signature here.

If the contract is broken you will immediately be told to leave and parents will be contacted. THERE WILL BE NO DRUGS OR ALCOHOL AT THE FORMAL. Thanks. The Formal Committee.

[Although she wasn't there, Anna's instructions were scrupulously carried out by her fellow students.]

Dear Best Bud,

Hey sweetie! Thanks for calling me back. I am in SOOO much pain. My period started today in the middle of my English exam! Do you know what? I think I might have the hots for L in our year. I know it sounds stupid but he has the most unusual intense look – he is the kind of guy I would like to get close to.

I swear that X is the biggest back stabber. She is sooo nice to people and then behind their backs she acts as if she hates them . . . [More of the same]

I told her not to be so negative and I decided to leave because I was bored. Do I sound like I'm gabbling to you? I am just squawking away. Are we going to the grand final together or have you already promised D? I wonder how much the tickets are and who will play. I reckon Manly and Newcastle will. That would be an excellent game. Can you read my writing? Sorry. I am lying in bed with my fluffy hot water bottle because my stomach is sore and I am very relaxed. Did you hear about J smashing the car? Yeah, you would have. Oh yeah, I've made a decision. There are no more drugs for you, only alcohol. It is getting tooo much. One day drugs will put an end to everything and that is a really depressing thought. Oh well, Sweetie, better go.

♡ you heaps, Anna.

The following diary entries were the last ones Anna made.

5.9.95
Dear Shefa,

My sickness is healing slowly, but surely. I just got back from the pictures. I saw All Men Are Liars. *It was excellent. I loved it. I could see it over and over again. I found out Alexia and I are spending Saturday together, without her boyfriend, I think.*

I have no man in my life at the moment. How come I never find anyone? All my friends have guys but me. Well, obviously I just don't have what it takes. One day hopefully the guy of my dreams will slide into my life.

I know I am only fifteen but I have a feeling my time on this earth is short. I suppose I should make the most of it. But I have a problem and that is I am too scared of everything, especially relationships. Maybe I should just relax. Who knows! Whatever happens, happens!

♡ always, Anna

24.9.95
Dear Shefa,

Hey, how are you? I am terrific. I have now learned to appreciate what I have and not pine over what I don't have. I know my views will probably change again soon. I have no love of my life at the moment.

. . . Maybe one day I will be beautiful. I know I am not ugly but I am not all that pretty. I am not fat – but I am not skinny. I really want to write a poem for you. What should I base it around – friends? . . . Males? Oh by the way at this point in my life the male gender means everything to me.

I have noticed lately that I have actually matured a bit. Even though when I'm in a hype I am still extremely immature, my thoughts have changed and I actually think before I speak.

Anyway. Write soon. Anna.

In November 1995, Angela dreamed about her daughter for the first time since her death. She was in a waiting room at an almost deserted railway station when Anna came in the door. It was a cold spring day; Anna was wearing a jumper over her summer school uniform. As Angela hurried towards the girl, Anna strode forward to meet her mother, her lovely smile lighting her face with pleasure. Angela desperately embraced her daughter and held her tight. This contact with her child's sweet tactile flesh was what she missed; this was what she needed most.

After a long time Anna drew back and gazed into her mother's face. "I came to tell you that I'm all right," she said. "I want you to know that I'm happy, Mum. But I'm very busy. I have a lot of work to do here." She smiled again and then walked away, leaving by another door. Angela watched her daughter go but knew she should not follow.

Angela has not dreamed about Anna again.

For Anna Victoria Wood, the summer of ninety-five never came. Yet in the changing seasons of her fifteen years on earth, she created more joy and happiness than many people manage in three-score years and ten.

Born in the arms of winter, she blossomed into loveliness in the spring. There she remains, forever a teenage child swaying on the edge of life's miracle.

EPILOGUE

It was dark outside where the parents had gathered to collect their children, but the primary school hall was full of fluorescent light and laughter.

"It's time, it's time!" the kids shouted and the teachers nodded and grinned and slid another CD disc into the ghetto-blaster on the stage.

As the new music filled the hall the girls and boys moved out into the centre and began dancing to a different beat.

They danced in irregular lines, without partners, alone but in time, slowly at first, then faster as the grinding thud of the techno music caught at their feet and drove them into rhythms of their own creation.

They danced and danced. Boys and girls alike executed swift neat manoeuvres involving hips, legs and feet, twisting and turning, hitting their heels, jumping, turning, jerking around and starting the whole routine again.

There wasn't any counting.

They danced and danced. Somebody turned down the lights and all that was visible in the spotlight from the stage was the glow of white clothing and the flash of their teeth as they smiled.

The music pounded. The grown-ups fell back into the darkness and watched in wonder as their graceless and awkward children, now as mechanical as well-oiled machines, performed routines they'd never known.

"What is this?" asked an Asian father. "I don't understand. This doesn't look like school dancing."

In the dark it wasn't clear if his neighbour was a parent or a teacher. It didn't really matter.

"We've shown them the way we do it," she said. "They've tried it our way.

"They're starting to grow up. Now it's their turn to choose."

The children's faces gleamed with sweat and power. Their eyes shone. Eighty bodies leapt in the air, landed with a shuddering thud, spun and turned around and away from their patiently waiting parents.

They danced on.

HELP LINES

ALL STATES:
Lifeline (24 hours, 7 days a week)
131 114 (cost of a local call)

Kids' Help Line (24 hour)
1800 551 800 (free call)

www.reachout.asn.au

New South Wales:
Alcohol and Drug Information Service (02) 9361 8000
[24 hours] 1800 422 599

Salvo Care Lines:
Care Line (02) 9331 6000
Crisis Line (02) 9331 2000
Youth Line (02) 9360 3000

Victoria:
Direct Line (Drug and Alcohol Counselling Information and
    Referral Service) (03) 9416 1818
[24 hours] 1800 136 385

Queensland:
Alcohol and Drug Information Service (07) 3236 2414
[24 hours] 1800 177 833

Salvation Army Bridge Program (07) 3369 0922

South Australia:
Alcohol and Drug Information Service 13 1340
[24 hours]

Drug and Alcohol Services Council (08) 8274 3333
[9 a.m. – 5 p.m. Monday – Friday]
Western Australia:
Alcohol and Drug Information Service (08) 9442 5000
[24 hours] 1800 198 024

Salvo Care Line (08) 9227 8655

Northern Territory:
Amity House (Community Drug and Alcohol Services, Darwin)
(089) 8981 8030
[8.30 a.m. – 4.30 p.m. Monday – Friday] 1800 629 683

Australian Capital Territory:
Alcohol and Drug Program, ACT Health (02) 6205 4545

Drug Referral and Information Centre (02) 6248 7677

Salvation Army Bridge Program (02) 6295 1256

RECOMMENDED READING

Dr David Bennett, *Growing Pains: What to Do When Your Children Turn into Teenagers,* Doubleday, new edition 1995.

Steve and Shaaron Biddulph, *The Making of Love: How to Stay in Love as a Couple Through Thick and Thin (Even with Kids!),* Doubleday, republished 1992.

Dr Simon Clarke and Elizabeth Kelly, *Taming Your Teenager,* part of the Bantam Health Book Series, Gore & Osment, 1995.

Terry Colling and Janet Vickers, *Teenagers: A Guide to Understanding Them,* Bantam Books, 1988. Available in libraries only.

Dr Moira Eastman, *Family: The Vital Factor,* Collins Dove, Melbourne, 1989. Available in libraries only.

M. Palin, *Drugs and Your Teenager: A "Don't Panic" Guide for Australian Parents*, Maxibooks, Springwood, 1993.